SECRETS OF MIDNIGHT

Chronicles of Midnight Book 3
DEBBIE CASSIDY

Cover by Covers by Julie

The assembly room slowly filled with humans. The district council had provided cheap plastic chairs that scraped over the floor as attendees seated themselves. Langley, the head of the MED, stood by the entrance that would admit the chief council members, his lips turned down in disapproval. Several other MED officers dotted the room—a precaution, just in case proceedings got volatile.

"This is your fault," Bane grumbled.

Urgh, this again. I rolled my eyes. "I do not control the minds of humans. Not one of my skill sets."

He made a harrumph sound. "You should have shut her down immediately. As soon as she came to you with the preposterous idea."

"It's not preposterous to want to take your fate in your own hands, to want to protect yourself."

He made a sound of exasperation in the back of his throat. "They're humans. Fragile, mortal beings, easily crushed, chewed up, and spat out."

"All the more reason to give them the power to fight back. Come on. You must see the benefits for Midnight if humans could fight back against the scourge and The Breed."

He sighed, his powerful chest rising and falling, stretching the fabric of his shirt so taut I was afraid it would tear under the strain at any moment.

"Seriously? Do you get your clothes custom-made?"

He shot me an are-you-fucking-kidding-me look.

I shrugged. "It's a reasonable question."

The humans had settled down, waiting eagerly for the proceedings to commence. Bane and I leaned up against the wall opposite Langley, halfway down the room. The door beside Langley swung open, and five humans came striding in. They climbed up onto the podium at the front of the chamber and settled down behind a long desk. It all looked very official, but it was a farce, because how the heck were they gonna stop the kind of movement that one woman was starting—a movement that I was totally behind, by the way, and if I was honest, I was developing a serious crush on the instigator of this event.

The doors at the back of the room slammed open, and the woman in question entered. Ava strode in, tall, blonde, and defiant, her head held high. This was the woman who'd fought back against Dorian, who'd broken his compulsion and moved me to help liberate the contracted humans from House Vitae's grasp. It had been almost six weeks since that day, but we'd been in contact ever since, and she'd come to me over a week ago with this idea, this venture that was a passion shining in her emerald eyes. Man, how she'd changed from the scrawny thing Dorian had been feeding from. She'd put the weight back on, turned it into muscle, and was looking pretty kick-ass in the threads I'd helped her pick out for the event. The boots were kick-the-shit-outta-you hot, and the leather jacket was just sexy. Eight other humans walked behind her, dressed in black, hair slicked and coiffed, and looking dangerous. Yeah, they certainly looked the part they were asking permission to play — a human Protectorate. Fuck the MED who sat behind desks and pushed paper. Fuck waiting for the MPD to show up to save the day. No. These humans wanted to take action, and damn, I needed pom-poms and a cheerleader outfit real bad right about now.

I recognized several faces, all humans that had been held hostage by Dorian and his Sanguinata. They knew what it was like to feel truly powerless, and they were here to demand authority to do something about it. They wanted to form a unit, to train with the MPD, and work alongside us in keeping Midnight safe. Bane, being Bane, was less than impressed. He saw it as having to babysit humans while trying to save all the other humans. The man was most definitely a glass-half-empty guy.

But empowering the humans was surely the way forward? And if we were all about the free will, then surely we needed to support the humans in this.

Ava walked past us, dropping me a wink on her way to the front of the room.

Bane snorted in disgust. "Yep, this is your fault."

Okay, so maybe I'd encouraged her a smidge. But where was the harm in that? In my humble opinion, there should be no need for jumping through hoops. If humans wanted to band together and form a unit to fight back against the terrors of Midnight, then fair play to them. I was all about the empowerment, and Bane could carry on looking like he'd sucked on Lilith's sour tits for all I cared.

"The council won't approve it," he said smugly.

"God, you sound like that wanker, Langley. They can't stop us from moving forward with this."

"Us?"

"I'm helping no matter what the outcome."

"Of course you are, Harker," he said dryly. "Because insubordination means nothing to you, does it? Why don't you teach them that, eh? And then watch them get killed, because a unit is only as good as its chain of command."

Ouch. He had a point. Time to swallow my pride. "I'd like to help them regardless, if that's all right with you, boss."

"We'll see."

Was that a smile tugging at the corner of his mouth?

The room fell into silence, and the central council member, a somber-looking, middle-aged woman, began to speak.

"Ava Love, you have petitioned the council for the authority to form a defense unit made up of humans. Is this correct?"

"Yes, ma'am," Ava said.

The councilwoman scanned a piece of paper on the desk before her. "Permission to use lethal force against hostile nephilim, including, but not limited to, the scourge and The Breed."

"Yes."

"And you state that you have the support of the MPD in this endeavor?" She glanced across at Bane, who remained impassive.

I nudged him sharply in the ribs, and with an exasperated sigh, he nodded.

The councilwoman turned her attention back to Ava. "Miss Love, you are asking the council to permit you to put your life and the lives of your fellow humans at risk."

"It's better than being powerless and getting picked off every month," Ava replied tersely.

The councilwoman's lips tightened. "It is also extremely dangerous, like agreeing to send a group of lambs into wolf territory. So, tell me why should we grant such a petition?"

Ava crossed her arms under her breasts. "With all due respect to the council, this is merely a formality that the MPD insisted I go through. Whether you give your permission or not, we, as the citizens of Midnight, have the right to protect ourselves."

Oh, man. This was specifically what I'd advised her against. Ava Love had a tendency to get mouthy, and her recent stint as Dorian's blood bag had lit a fire of vengeance and determination inside her that could easily flare out of control. It was one of the reasons why, when she'd come to me asking for help on this project, I'd agreed. She was a laser without a focus, a weapon without a target. Yeah, she needed this, but challenging the authority of the council was a dumb move, and the downturn of the councilwoman's mouth told me she was about to deliver a smackdown.

It was time to step in, but a member of the public beat me to it.

"And what if your actions rile up The Breed and the scourge?" a young, heavily pregnant woman said. Her face flushed, whether with embarrassment of all the eyes on her or in indignation, I wasn't sure. "What if the change prompts them to increase their attacks on Midnight? Why try to fix what's working? The MPD and the MED have been keeping us safe for years. The Houses provide ample protection during scourge runs and from The Breed."

Ava's shoulders tensed.

Bane snorted. It was his *I told you so* snort. The man didn't have to speak to communicate his annoyance, derision, or disappointment. He had snorts to do that for him, and the fact that I could decipher them was kind of worrying.

The councilwoman waved the pregnant lady down, but a man at the back stood up. "She's right. This is the last thing we need. We have things under control. The casualties are minimal. Why rock the boat?"

The councilwoman raised her brows and sat back. "Well, Miss Love, would you care to respond?"

Ava pressed her lips together, her eyes flashing dangerously. She turned to face the crowd. "Why rock the boat?" Her tone was incredulous. "This isn't a boat, this is our home, and we need to stand up and protect it. The MPD can only do so much. They can't be everywhere at once. Have any of you stopped to wonder how hard it must be for them to cover the whole district every month when the scourge attacks?" She focused on the guy. "Minimal casualties doesn't cut it. There should be zero casualties, and with our help, the MPD may be able to achieve that. I'm done being a victim, and it's about time you stopped thinking like one too."

A low murmur skittered over the crowd and several heads began to nod in agreement. The councilwoman's lips twitched.

Bane sighed. "Damn it."

"Ava Love, the council grants you authority to form a unit, but active duty will only commence once the MPD has signed off on your training."

Langley's face was a picture of incredulousness.

The councilwoman scrawled something on the paper and then held it out to Ava. "There you go, Miss Love. I look forward to hearing about your progress. It's about time we made some changes in Midnight. Less paperwork and more action." She slid a glance Langley's way, and his eyes narrowed.

Ha. Looked like I'd misjudged the councilwoman and the council, but for once, I was glad about being wrong.

The council representatives filed out and Langley followed, probably eager to try and change their minds. It wasn't that he disagreed with the unit. It was more the fact that its existence made the MED look bad. Like, why hadn't they come up with this idea? Or why was it necessary in the first place?

Ava strolled toward us, her face alight with excitement. "Did you hear that?"

Bane pushed off the wall and brushed past her. Damn, he was so not happy. He'd probably been banking on the council shutting this down. Great. I'd have to soothe the bear. Shame he didn't like honey.

"You did great, Ava."

She winced. "I almost blew it, didn't I?"

"Yeah, but you pulled it back."

"So, when can we start training?"

"Come by tomorrow. We'll make a start. The scourge runs again in three weeks. I think we can have you ready by then."

"Why not today?"

I glanced over her shoulder at the door that Bane had just pushed through. "I have a few things to sort out first."

She followed my gaze. "Boss still not completely on board, eh?"

I winced. "Sorry."

She pushed back her shoulders. "Well, we'll just have to show him that we mean business."

Yeah, and I needed to make sure he was going to be there to see it.

Bane laid his cards on the table. "Gin," he said smugly.

I threw my carefully constructed set onto the table in a huff. That was four games in a row. "I actually hate you. You know it doesn't count as a win if you skim my mind, right?"

He leaned back in his seat, arms laid across the back of the sofa, powerful thighs spread wide. For a moment, I considered hopping over the coffee table, scaling his massive frame, straddling those hips, yanking back that head, and — stop it. My demon shrugged. *Honey, that was all you,* her voice, now my conscience, whispered.

Oh, shit. I dropped my attention to the table. Had he read my thoughts?

"I didn't skim your mind, Harker," Bane said softly. "I never do. However, sometimes your thoughts are pretty loud. And when we get intimate, they're impossible to ignore."

He said it casually, as if we got up close and personal every day, which we so didn't. This, playing cards in the lounge, was as intimate as shit had gotten the past few weeks. I'd opted to feed off Rivers and Orin the last few times. Bane's power sustained me longer, but frankly, I didn't trust myself not to jump his bones during the process.

And that would be fine, the demon said. Where was Ambrosius when you needed a male smackdown? Right now, I'd take him over the feminine and sultry, carnal-whispering demon any day.

Bane gathered the cards and shuffled them. The others would be back from patrol soon, and then we'd have our weekly meeting. Scourge had gotten out of hand recently, attacking solo or in pairs outside of runs. Sector three was getting the brunt of it, and we'd had to start sending out Protectorate without a primary in charge. There'd been several command promotions in the works. It was the only option, because, damn, even nephs needed sleep.

I'd alternated between working with Bane or Ryker and had even gone solo with my own team on several occasions. With Drayton gone and Cassie shirking her duties, we were severely undermanned. Another reason why having a human unit out there helping out was a good idea.

Bane dropped the cards on the table and

sauntered over to the drinks tray, where he poured a triple shot and downed it.

"You want one?" Bane asked.

"Sure."

He brought over a glass and then watched as I downed it, his intense gaze on my throat as it bobbed. The alcohol didn't do anything in terms of intoxication, but it tasted good going down.

"When did you last feed?" His voice was suddenly rough.

Last night, courtesy of Rivers. My pulse spiked as I considered lying, but he'd know soon enough once we began the exchange. But fuck, if he carried on looking at me like that I'd risk it just to get my hands on him. A wicked laugh filled my head, and I closed my eyes, blocking out his feral features and willing my pulse to stop doing the bloody fandango.

"I'm good."

He scanned my face and then turned away, muttering what sounded suspiciously like the word *shame*. It was one of those moments, the tingling, tense ones that part of me wanted to push into dangerous waters, and the other sane part struggled to steer clear of, because my gut told me that launching myself off that cliff would mean a forever freefall that I wasn't prepared for no matter how much my body longed for it.

Time for a change of subject. "Oleander's

settling in well."

Bane snorted. "If you call sleeping in a bed I provided and eating our food *settling in* then yes."

"Hey, it's not too bad. He *has* taken over kitchen duty."

Bane refilled his glass and sipped this time. "There is that."

I bit back a smile. "It's a shame that you won't get to wear your apron for a while, though."

He shot me an irritated look. "It's a practical necessity. Cooking can be messy, not to mention spitting oil when you fry shit."

I widened my eyes innocently. "Of course. And the frills give it just the right homey touch."

He leaned up against the hearth and ignored the jibe. "At least he's stopped crying."

"Yeah, that was a rough couple of weeks."

And then he'd discovered human literature and Orin's special cookbook, and I had to say, the ancient had some serious culinary skills.

"At least the damn library is getting some use," Bane pointed out.

We fell into silence. With the change in topic exhausted, there was once again that sizzling elephant in the room, the one chanted, *fuck, fuck, fuck.* Maybe that's what we needed to do. Just bang and get it out of the way. We'd built up the expectation, this weird dynamic through our feedings that needed to be satisfied, and then maybe we could just move on. But every time this thought popped into my head, an icy hand closed itself over my heart and Drayton's face came to mind, accompanied by the whispered thought, *But what if it doesn't?*

The slam of the front door signaled the arrival of the others.

Ryker and Orin strode into the room, trailed by Rivers. Their clothes were torn, their faces bloody. Orin staggered as he stepped over the threshold, and Ryker grabbed hold of him. I was out of my seat in a shot, bracing the mammoth as best I could on the opposite side.

Rivers limped over to the sofa and sat down, stretching out a blood-soaked leg wrapped in shredded jeans.

"What the fuck happened?" Bane asked.

"The Breed," Ryker ground out. "The fuckers ambushed us while we were taking out a couple of rippers."

"It was a set-up," Rivers said. "I'm sure of it. The rippers lured us into an alley and then the fucking Breed attacked."

My pulse kicked up. The Breed had lain low for weeks, and goodness knew, I'd searched for them. I had a score to settle with Max, their leader—we all did. Because of him, Drayton was gone, and now they'd made an appearance, and not just any appearance, a coordinated attack. The state of the boys made sense because they'd fought back, not as MPD on patrol, but as three guys looking for revenge. They'd fought dirty, and it showed.

"Did you see Max?" My throat was tight. "Was he there?"

"No," Rivers said tightly. His silver eyes flashed cold and deadly. "I looked."

"We took out four at least, but the others got away." Orin's tone was saturated with regret. He winced as Ryker and I lowered him into the wingback. "I'm sorry. We wanted to grab a live one."

And they'd fucking tried. I placed a hand on Orin's shoulder. "Don't be sorry. I'm just glad you're all right."

Bane grabbed the first aid kit from the unit under the window. It was a huge, decked-out kit—a mini emergency arsenal—and over the past few weeks we'd dipped into it often. Ryker healed the worst wounds with his mojo. But for minor injuries, the kit worked fine, especially as we healed pretty fast on our own anyway.

The past month had shown a spike in all kinds of supernatural activity. The rippers and suckers had changed the rules, attacking when they pleased, in twos and threes. Tristan had reported a spike in accident and emergency patients, all victims of supernatural attacks, and not just from the usual suspects.

Arachne, the cursed spider woman, had been right. Something was coming—a whole lot of crap from the outside, to be precise. The most recent was a spate of hauntings across sector two. Midnight didn't have ghosts; we had the Respite cemetery and the souls trapped there, and that was it. The rest of the dead, well, they went wherever the dead go. A question not even Bane could answer, and one I'd made a note to ask the Black Wings about next time our paths crossed. In the meantime, there was little the MPD could do to combat the fresh wave of ghouls to the district. Hopefully they'd get bored and move on to wherever ghosts are meant to go. If not, then we'd have to investigate further, find some kind of fix, because, yeah, you guessed it, the MED had shoved those cases right in our laps.

I took the kit from Bane and began to patch up Rivers. His jeans had to be cut away first, and then the wound cleaned. Shit, the gash in his calf was deep. He didn't even flinch when I applied the antiseptic, although the sting must have been a bitch. Did the guy have no pain receptors? I worked fast, applying gauze and wrapping the wound in a bandage.

"Thank you." He smiled thinly.

He looked pale, probably through loss of blood if the soaked denim was anything to go on. Next up was the bulky roan with the head wound that was still bleeding. It was impossible to tell how deep it was without getting close enough to examine it properly, but making him move around probably wasn't a great idea.

There was only one way to do it. Using the wingback's arms to kneel on, I straddled Orin and gently tilted his chin to take a proper look at the wound. He closed his eyes, breathing deep. This close up, his lashes were thick fans resting on his crimson-spattered cheeks. Not even the blood could mar his beauty. How had I never noticed? He opened his eyes, his pupils dilating like twin inky pools surrounded by an ocean of deep blue.

"How bad is it?" His chest rumbled against my palm. "Stitches bad?"

"Yeah." I hated doing stitches. I broke eye contact in favor of Ryker. "You think you could fix him up?"

Ryker nodded. His lips were pale and drawn. "I've got this."

I climbed off Orin and walked over to the drinks tray to prepare drinks for the guys, but Bane was already on it. He handed me a glass and jerked his head in Rivers's direction. Rivers accepted the amber liquid and took a tentative sip. He wasn't much of a boozer unless it was medicinal. Right now, he looked like he could do with a splint to hold him upright. He must be in pain, but Rivers wasn't the kind to show it. Even when I fed off him, he kept his distance, extending an arm and then averting his gaze. If I didn't know better, I'd think he didn't like me siphoning him, but the fact that he would seek me out and offer contradicted that impression.

He looked up at me now, his pale eyes all pupil.

I smoothed back his hair and pressed a chaste kiss to his forehead. "You'll live."

He graced me with his signature lopsided smile and took another sip.

Ryker finished healing Orin and then slumped onto the sofa beside Rivers. He pressed a hand over his abdomen. Wait, was he hurt too?

"Ryker? Let me see." I went to pull up his shirt, but he gripped my wrist tight, halting me.

"It's fine."

His fingers were cold, and his brow was beaded in perspiration. He was *so* not fine. I grit my teeth and stared him down. "Let. Me. See."

"Let her examine you," Bane ordered sternly.

Ryker pressed his head back against the sofa and slowly relinquished his grip on my arm. Now that I was looking, the pain etched into his face was evident. His T-shirt was black, which was probably why none of us had noticed that it was fucking soaked in blood, and as I peeled it back, Bane let out a triple curse.

"Fucking hell, Ryker."

There was a dime-sized hole in his side, but no hole in the shirt. "How?"

"Exit wound," Ryker said. "The pole entered from behind but never pierced the front of the shirt. I'm working on healing it. Just clean it up and cover it, please."

My hands shook as I patched him up, and

my eyes burned in their sockets. He'd been hurt, and I'd made him expend energy to fix Orin, whose wound could have been stitched manually if I hadn't been so fucking squeamish. Ryker always seemed so together, so untouchable, that it never occurred to me that he could be hurt too. It would be like having to patch up Bane and check for wounds. Those two were the invincible giants of the team, while Orin was the gentle giant and Rivers … well, I still hadn't wrapped my mind around him yet.

Ryker ran a hand over my head. "I'll be fine."

I locked gazes with him. "You better be."

Bane handed him a drink, and Ryker downed it.

"Look at us," Orin said, his tone laced with bitterness. "We're getting our arses kicked out there. The rules are changing, and we have no idea what game we're playing. We need more officers."

I parked my ass on the edge of the sofa that housed Rivers and Ryker. "Which is why we need to do what we can to get Ava and the human unit up to speed."

I glanced at Bane, expecting him to argue, to make some cutting or sarcastic comment about humans being weak, and blah, blah, blah, but he had his hands on his hips, chin tucked in, and was ominously silent.

"When does the training start?" Rivers

asked.

"Tomorrow."

"I'll come and help; my legs should be healed by then."

"No," Bane said.

Here we go.

"Harker and I will take care of it."

Okay. Was not expecting that. Bane met my gaze, and I scrambled to hide my surprise.

"Orin is right," Bane continued. "The rules *have* changed, and it's time to try a different approach. We need boots on the ground. We need to be prepared for anything. And if those humans are going to be fighting alongside us, then they deserve the best training we can offer."

Ryker raised his glass. "Hear, hear."

About fucking time.

Bane took his usual spot by the hearth, the flames casting fiery shadows across his cutthroat face. "There is something else I wanted to let you all know." This time his attention was on Orin. "I've decided to fire Cassie."

Orin flinched as if he'd been slapped.

Bane's jaw tightened. He was probably expecting opposition, but Orin merely closed his eyes for a long beat, shoulders rising and falling in a sigh. "Go for it."

Bane nodded curtly. "Good. Next time she drops by for a change of clothes, send her my way."

It was the right call. Cassie wasn't one of us

anymore, hadn't been for weeks now—bailing on patrol again and again until we simply stopped scheduling her onto the rota. But firing her was the final nail in the coffin of her relationship with Orin. She'd made her decision to be with Killion, but it was obvious that Orin had hoped she'd change her mind and come home. As long as she'd still been a member of the Protectorate, there'd been a chance of that happening.

Orin pushed up out of his seat. "I'm going to get some shut-eye."

If he'd been human, I'd have warned him about sleeping so soon after an injury, but nephs didn't get concussions. He took a step and swayed.

"Whoa." I grabbed hold of him and ducked under his arm. "Let me help you."

Orin leaned into me. "Great. Now I feel totally manly."

Ryker snort-chuckled.

"Drop him off and head back," Bane said. "We still have shit to discuss." He looked to Orin. "I'll fill you in tomorrow. Get some rest."

We made it up to Orin's room without incident, but he was unsteady, and by the time we got to his bed he was leaning on me a little too heavily. I was strong, but he was a big dude. We got him onto the bed, and then I plonked my ass on the edge of his mattress.

"You going to be okay?"

He closed his eyes. "I'll have to be."

Man, my heart ached for him. "It will get easier with time."

He chuckled, but it was a humorless sound. "It would help if she just made up her mind."

"What do you mean? She left. That's kinda indicative of a mind made up."

He opened his eyes, and the pain swimming in the azure depths was nothing to do with the head injury. "Last time she was here, we made love. I thought we were good. And then she left again."

Heat flared in my chest, indignation and anger mingling to make a dangerous cocktail.

"I'm an idiot, aren't I?" he asked.

Oh, man. If anyone was the idiot, it was Cassie, the fucking whore. "No, Orin. You're a good guy. A fucking great one." On impulse, I leaned in and pressed a soft kiss to the corner of his mouth. "She doesn't deserve you."

He gazed up at me searchingly. "I wish I could stop loving her."

"Love's a bitch, all right." I leaned back. "Which is why I plan to steer clear."

I'd almost slipped up with Drayton. And Bane was getting too close. The desire to just abandon myself to fate and let my heart guide me was a sweet temptation that was getting stronger the more time I spent in Midnight, the longer I remained a part of this close-knit group of nephs. In fact, I was probably a little in love with them all.

Orin's lips quirked in an ironic smile. "Love is the hook that keeps us suspended above the tumultuous waters of despair. It anchors us in the storm of devastation that is constantly sweeping across this district. Love is the only weapon we have against the monsters that lurk in the darkness of Midnight."

A shiver ran up my spine. "Very poetic." I kept my tone light, not wanting him to see how affected I'd been by his beautiful words.

Twin spots of color appeared high on his cheekbones, and he shrugged. "I like words."

Who would have pegged him for a poet? "Well, here are some useful words for you — get some sleep."

He smiled and closed his pretty eyes.

I sat with him until his breathing evened out. He didn't deserve to be treated this way. I'd meant what I'd said, Cassie didn't deserve him, and it was about time someone delivered a smackdown.

And that someone was going to be me.

Jacket on, I headed for the door, wanting to get to Cassie before I lost the fire smoldering in my belly.

"Harker, where the fuck do you think you're going?" Bane barked from the lounge archway. "I already briefed Ryker and Rivers, you took so bloody long. Get in here so I can fill you in on the plan for the next few weeks."

Oh shit, he still wanted to discuss stuff. "I was headed out. Can it wait?"

He arched a brow. "Are you fucking kidding me? Would I be waiting for you if it could wait? And were you planning on getting wherever you wanted to go on foot?"

Dammit, I really needed to learn to drive, but then, light-bulb moment. "You could drive me, and then you could brief me on the way?" I gave him a hopeful cheesy smile.

He rolled his eyes. "Fine. Get in the van. I'll be there in a minute."

Five minutes later we were driving out of the gates and into the night.

"Where to?" Bane asked.

"The Deep."

His hands tightened on the wheel. "I assume this isn't a social call."

"You assume right."

"Sometimes I wonder why you care so damned much."

He knew what I was planning. How the heck was he always on the same wavelength as me? "Yeah, well, I'd rather care too much than not enough. If more people cared, this city would be a safer place to live."

"Cassie has always been selfish," Bane said. "But I didn't expect her to be cruel. Not to Orin. Not like this. And to shirk her duties ... it's not like her. Not at all."

"I don't know her well enough to judge, I just know that it's killing Orin, and that's something I can't allow to happen." I turned my head to watch the dark street slide by, slick with recent rain and dotted with tiny puddles.

"The next few weeks I want you focusing on Ava and her unit," Bane said. "We need them up to scratch by the next scourge run."

"If there is one."

He snorted. "Yeah, they're attacking independently so frequently I'm wondering that too. But we need to be prepared. I've reduced your patrol, but I'd like you to take the human unit out a couple of times, just so they can see how we do things. I've paired you with Ryker and Orin for those patrols."

My heart sank a little. "I thought *we* were partners now." I injected a light tone into my voice.

He flicked a glance my way, and his mouth curved. "No, Harker. I'm not your partner. I'm your boss."

Oookay. "Anything else you want to brief me on."

We rolled down the road toward the beach and The Deep. The grumble of angry waves crashing against the cliffs to the east surrounded us.

"Keep your cool."

It was my turn to smile. "Like a cucumber."

We pulled up in the car park.

"You need me to come in with you?" Bane asked.

"Why? Do you *want* to hold my hand?"

His brows flicked up, and the silence stretched out between us.

Awkward. "Um. No. I'm good."

Leaving him in the van, I hopped out and headed for the neon-bathed entrance. She probably wasn't here, in which case I'd have made a wasted trip, but I really hoped she was.

It was a slow night, barely any patrons, and hardly any humans. Jonah caught my eye as I entered and ushered me over to the bar.

"Hey. It's dead in here tonight."

He frowned. "Business hasn't been great recently. The increased ripper and sucker activity means humans haven't been venturing out, and no humans means fewer neph."

Oh shit. "I'm sorry. We're doing everything we can to keep the district safe."

"I know you are. We heard about the council meeting—the human who wants to set up a unit to fight back."

"You did?"

"Yes, and it's caused quite a stir in the sea dweller communities."

Okay, I was intrigued. "What kind of stir?"

"Well, up until now, it's been nephs keeping humans safe, but the Protectorate isn't enough any longer. And it shames some of the prouder nephs that humans, the weaker species, are rising up to act as protector while the neph community sits back and does nothing."

My chest fluttered with hope. "What are you saying?"

"I'm saying *we* want to help too. We can't venture too far from the sea, but we can form a coastal patrol unit."

"We? As in the kelpies?"

He made a disgusted sound in the back of his throat. "The kelpies care for nothing but themselves. But the sirens and the roan wish to help, and there are others, ancient ones, who will lend their support, if needed. There are rumblings of change, of a new darkness that is seeping into our city."

"You mean the hauntings?"

His brows snapped down. "No. Not the ghosts. This is something else. Something very old and very powerful. The ancient sea dwellers feel it, and it scares them. And trust me, they do not scare easily." He wiped the bar with a cloth even though it was immaculate. "Tell Bane. Tell him what we plan to do. Tell him the coast will be safe."

Jonah's wife came sashaying toward us from the other end of the bar. He turned to her, his worried frown melting away into a warm smile.

He slipped his arm around her, pulled her to his side, and kissed the top of her head. Man, she was dinky compared to him, and they looked so sweet together.

She looked up at him. "And what were you two gossiping about? It looked pretty intense."

"I was telling the officer about our coastal guard plan," Jonah said.

Her expression sobered. "We have to do something to help. The neph who frequent this place can't deny it any longer. They see the humans have stopped coming here, and they know why. Many of them will join us for purely selfish reasons, but it doesn't matter, as long as we get enough nephs to keep the coast safe from attacks."

"I'll let Bane know. And thank you for taking it upon yourselves to set this up."

Jonah's attention slipped over my head. "Your Protectorate friend just walked in. I assume that's who you've come looking for. She's in here most evenings with Killion and his cronies."

My spine stiffened. "Thanks."

Cassie had taken a spot at a corner table, the same table where Ryker and I had found her several weeks ago when she'd first left us for Killion. She was alone this time, probably waiting on the others. Taking a deep breath, I sauntered over.

She looked up as my shadow fell over her. Her brows flicked up, and her gaze slipped behind me.

"You're here alone?" she said.

"I need to speak to you."

Her face went blank for a moment.

"Cassie?"

She blinked and snapped, "Oh, for fuck's sake, more badgering? I told you last time I was at the mansion that I'd be back when I was ready."

Her facial expression, her attitude, and her tone all stoked the fire of indignation smoldering inside me. "I want you to leave Orin alone. Do not come back to the mansion, do not call, and don't try and see him again. You got that?"

She made an incredulous sound. "What the fuck? Are you hot for *him* now? Is that it? Drayton's been dead for less than two months, and you've already picked out your next conquest."

Oh, man. She was asking for a smack in the mouth. I took a step closer to her. "You really have a gutter mind, you know that? I actually thought you were cool when we first met. I thought we'd be friends, but I don't hang with heart-breaking, cheating bitches."

Her eyes narrowed and something dark passed over her face. "What happens between Orin and me has nothing to do with you. I love him, just like I love Killion."

"And that would be okay if Orin were happy to share you. But he isn't. You're hurting him. How can you not get that?"

For a moment, I thought I caught a glimpse of the old Cassie, the one that had laughed and joked with Orin in the kitchen over a scone. The one who'd trained me and stuck up for me with Bane. But the glimpse was fleeting, and the softness leeched from her eyes, leaving steel shadows in its place.

Her mouth twisted cruelly. "Fuck you, Harker. Orin is a big boy, and I mean big," she said suggestively. "And he's mine. He may not like it, but that's just the way it is." She shrugged. "I'm not going to chase him, but I'm Protectorate, and the mansion is my home. I can't help if our paths cross. If he comes to me with his huge puppy dog eyes, I'm not going to turn him down."

It was my turn to smile, and I could taste the self-satisfaction in my tone. "Just as well you're fired, then."

She blinked sharply. "You can't do that."

"No, she can't," Bane said, coming up behind me. The heat of his body skimmed up my spine.

Cassie shot me a smug look.

"But *I* can."

Her smile fell, and something in her demeanor shifted.

Bane's lip curled. "Don't come back, Cassie. If you do, the sentries will treat you as hostile, and they will rip you to shreds."

"You can't do this." She reached for his arm, but he shrugged her off.

"There is no room on my team for selfish bitches." His tone was even and matter-of-fact, which made it sting all the more.

"You're being impulsive. You need me, especially now that shit is hitting the fan out there."

"Hasn't seemed to bother you the past two weeks. And to be honest, we haven't really felt the loss. Harker makes up for it. She's ten times the neph you ever were."

Cassie opened and closed her mouth a couple of times, reminding me of a guppy.

"Let's get out of here." Bane gently gripped my elbow, sending a frisson of awareness through me. His words echoed in my ears, and a pleasant heat bloomed in my chest. In that moment, I'd have followed him to the ends of the earth.

"Did you mean what you said back there?"

He flicked a glance my way. "What? About firing Cassie?"

"No. The other thing?"

His lips twitched. "About not feeling her loss?"

He knew exactly what I was talking about. "No. The *other* thing. You know, about me being ten times the officer she was." There. I'd said it. "It sounded better when you said it, though."

He smiled, flashing fang that had me aching for something I didn't want to need.

"I meant it," he said. "But don't let it get to your head. Pride comes before a fall, and you're never too good to get tripped up. So, keep your eyes peeled, keep your wits about you, and be fucking smart."

I filled him in on what Jonah had said.

Bane turned off the main road and onto a slip that led to sector two. "Good. At least we can ease up on our coast patrols."

"We're not going back to base yet?"

"We're going to speak to a contact of mine about these hauntings. Get an insider view rather than an MED one. Then we're going to get some food. There's a great Thai restaurant on the outskirts of sector two." He cleared his throat. "If you're hungry."

My stomach rumbled. "I love Thai takeout. Shall I ring the others and see what they want us to pick up?"

He was silent, eyes fixed on the road, jaw tense. He looked pissed.

Wait a fucking minute. When he said we should eat, did he mean eat in, as in just him and me? The pulse in my throat did a drum roll. He wanted to have dinner with me? Bad move. Too intimate. Just him and me in a dimly lit restaurant with food, wine, and the back of a van. Bad move. Bad, bad move.

Do it, my demon whispered. *It's just food. Plus, he* is *the boss. Best to stay on his good side.*

We drove onto a residential street, and he brought the van to a halt with a shriek of rubber on asphalt, unbuckled his belt, and twisted in his seat to look at me.

"Are you hungry? Do you want to eat food with me? Just food, Harker. No wine, no intimacy, and no hot sex in the back of the fucking van."

Oh, shit. "You heard that?"

"Loud and clear." He leaned in. "Trust me,

Harker. When I fuck you for the first time, it most certainly won't be in the back of a van."

When, not *if.* He'd said *when.* And why was my brain short-circuiting right now?

He reached out and cupped the side of my face with his huge paw of a hand and ran the pad of his thumb across my bottom lip. "I know where your heart lies. I know it still hurts, and I know that our hearts and bodies can sometimes want different things. Sometimes, they can be greedy, and not all of us can separate our minds from our bodies. Take your time, but this thing we have, it isn't going away."

He'd said it. He'd actually said what we'd been skirting around all this time. Even when Drayton had been alive, this thing between us had been there, simmering and growing. The past few weeks with Drayton gone, Bane had become my crutch. Even with Ryker there to console me and counsel me, Bane had been the one to actively pull me out of the haze of depression by challenging me and giving me focus. And this attraction between us, this gnawing, gaping need, wasn't going to die an easy death, and I wasn't sure I wanted it to. I just wasn't ready to give in to it. It wasn't just because of Drayton. It was because of me. It was the block in my psyche; it was every fucking thing that could possibly go wrong.

Orin's words came to mind, his beautiful poetic prose about love being our only weapon, but this thing between Bane and me was nothing as tame as love. It was something volatile and dangerous, and damn, I wanted it.

There was no point in denying the truth. "I know."

He released me. "Good. Now let's go gather some intel."

We approached a silent, dark, two-story house, and climbed the steps to the porch to be greeted by a sweet little welcome mat and some of those wind chime things hanging from a hook in the awning. They tinkled in the chill breeze in the silence preceding Bane's knock on the door.

Seconds stretched by without response. Bane knocked again, and after a long minute, I peered through the frosted glass at the top of the front door—a pointless exercise, because it was pitch-black inside.

"Doesn't look like anyone is home."

Bane glanced over his shoulder. "No. He has to be home. His car is here. The man is a sloth. He drives everywhere, and he never ventures out after six p.m."

It was probably around nine p.m. now. "So, what do you suggest we do?"

He stepped off the porch. "I say we find a

way in."

"You want to break into his house?"

He gave me a flat look. "Yes, we break in if we have to. Something doesn't feel right."

I followed him around the side of the house, through a loosely-latched wooden gate, and into the backyard. Gooseflesh pricked my skin. Bane was right. Something *was* off, and the evidence smacked us in the face as we rounded the back of the structure. The rear door was hanging off its hinges, and one of the windows was smashed, leaving the net curtains billowing in the wind.

"Shit!" Bane ran into the building, boots crushing glass and debris.

Through the kitchen we went, past an upturned table and over smashed plates and cups. Bane ducked through the door into a hallway and climbed over a bookcase that had probably been yanked across the floor to stall a pursuer. Books littered the hardwood. Leather-bound titles, probably sourced from antique stores around the city. Oleander came to mind. How he'd love these books... and then shame colored my cheeks. The man who owned them was probably dead, and here I was coveting his damned collection for a friend.

We dashed up the stairs, our footsteps muffled by the thick carpet, and came to a standstill in front of a splintered door.

Bane took several slow breaths and then

skulked slowly toward the room. Weird how he was going all stealth mode now, once we'd practically bellowed our arrival. If something *was* still here, we'd pretty much announced our presence with the knock and then the barging in.

Bane stepped over the shattered white-washed wood and into the room beyond. A lamp flickered somewhere inside, casting eerie shadows on the opposite wall. Bane's huge frame blocked the entrance, and he let out a curse.

"What is it? What did you find?"

He walked farther into the room, and I followed to find carnage. What was once a study was now crimson-spattered chaos, and in the midst of it lay the broken, torn body of an elderly man.

Bane fell into a crouch by the body. "Oh, Jonathan, old friend." There was deep sorrow in those words—an intimacy that spoke of a lifetime of memories.

"Looks like a ripper attack." I moved around the body. "But it doesn't make sense. Rippers kill to feed. This is just a kill."

Jonathon's sightless eyes stared at us accusingly.

Bane reached out and closed the lids with his index finger and thumb. "This was a murder, plain and simple, and someone used a ripper to do it for them."

"But why? Why would someone want your

friend dead?"

Bane shook his head. "I don't know. Jonathan was a clairvoyant, a sensitive. I can't believe he didn't see this coming. That he didn't come to me."

I scanned the body, noting the cuts and bruises. He'd fought back, no doubt about that. One hand was contorted into a claw. The other was a fist. Wait. "Is he holding something?"

Bane gently opened Jonathan's hand and retrieved a screwed-up piece of paper. He smoothed it out and read the words scrawled on it.

I craned my neck to peer around his bicep. "What does it say?"

He shook his head. "It makes no sense. It says, *summon the piper.*"

"The piper? Who's that?"

Bane shrugged and pulled himself up to his full height, his lips downturned. "I'll call this in to the hospital and get Tristan to examine the body." He strode out of the room to make the call.

Jonathan had been a supernatural, so his death was ours to investigate, and from the look on Bane's face, he wasn't going to let this one end up in the cold case basket. The piper. There had to be some clue here as to what that meant? A notepad, a book, something. The desk had been knocked over, and pens and paper and notepads littered the floor. There could be a clue amongst the contents of his desk.

Bane returned to find me shoving everything from the desk into an emptied wastepaper bin.

His shoulder muscles rippled beneath his shirt as he crossed his arms. "You know this is a crime scene, right?"

"A supernatural crime scene. I doubt you're going to be taking fingerprints and checking blood types."

Bane didn't reply. His mournful gaze was once again fixed on his friend's dead body.

My heart ached for him. "How long did you know him?"

"Forever. I helped birth him. Jonathan was special. I should have called more often. Kept in touch."

There was a long story there, one he'd want to tell sometime soon, and one I'd want to hear, but the set of his jaw and the tension in his body screamed that now wasn't the time. We needed to focus on the case.

I held up the waste basket. "Maybe there's a clue to who this piper is in one of these notepads or books."

Bane crouched down again. "I'm sorry, old friend. If I could speak to you again, I'd tell you how much your friendship meant to me."

That was it! "You can."

"What?"

"You *can* speak to him again. He was killed

by a ripper, right?"

Bane's furrowed brow cleared. "The fucking cemetery."

"Bingo."

"Let's go."

There would be no Thai food today, but it no longer mattered, because my hunger had died. All that mattered was finding out who had killed Bane's friend and thrown a shroud of sorrow over my boss.

Bane parked the van in front of the cemetery arch but didn't make a move to get out. Instead, he sat staring at the ivy that crawled over the iron, weaving in and out to make a barrier all of its own.

I turned in my seat to face him. "When was the last time you came here?"

"I can't recall." His tone was hushed, reverent. "Probably when it was first formed." He sat back in his seat. "It feels like forever ago."

"Who did you come to see?"

He blinked as if coming out of a trance. "It doesn't matter. She's long gone now."

She? A lover, a friend? I tamped down on the questions. Whoever she was, the mausoleum, and the world beyond, would have claimed her by now. She'd have forgotten herself, her memories of life, and to her, death would be her new life. I guess it was Arcadia's version of an afterlife. But hang on a second … hadn't someone told me that in order to forget, you had to be forgotten. I opened my mouth to pose this question, but Bane chose that moment to unlock the door and jump out.

Should I go with him? Did he want a moment alone?

He slammed his door then leaned in against the window. "Come on, Harker. We haven't got all night."

Okay, this was my cue to exit, but my hand faltered on the door. The last time I'd been here it had been to tell Drayton's dead human lover that he'd been killed. The memory hit me sudden and swift, knocking the breath from my lungs and leaving me dizzy for a moment.

"Harker?" Bane's voice was like a blast of icy air, shaking off the lingering cobwebs of that memory.

I joined him under the archway, and together we stepped through into the domain of the dead. The moonlight here was brighter, the air lighter, and the fireflies frolicked amongst the gravestones, making halos of green-tinged light around the stone. The mausoleum sat squat and inviting, the door slightly ajar and hanging with ivy. Lilting music—a love ballad, a nostalgic tune—drifted out to greet us. It wrapped around me, taking me by the throat and whispering, *Enter, come see the delights on the other side.*

I took an involuntary step toward the

structure.

"Harker," Bane snapped. "No."

"What?"

"You need an invite. Did Drayton not tell you that?"

He hadn't, but someone else had — a male ghost whose name escaped me, but one who'd had an obvious fondness for Drayton's ex. I shook my head to clear the haze and locked my knees. No going into the mausoleum without an invite. Got it.

"Jonathan. Are you here, old friend?" Bane walked around the nearest headstone. "We need to talk."

Silence greeted us, but the fireflies rose up in a glowing veil and hovered over the mausoleum like a neon shroud. And then the veil parted and a familiar, plump figure stepped through. It was the mother of the man Drayton and I had returned to the cemetery; Maurice, or Maury, or something, his name had been.

She cocked her head, her eyes flaring in surprise at the sight of Bane. "You know our newest arrival."

Bane inclined his head. "Doris. It's nice to see you after so long. You're still as beautiful as ever."

She let out a bark of laughter. "Still the silver-tongued devil, I see." But she fingered her rigidly styled sixties hair, preening just a bit.

Bane smiled, his eyes crinkling with

warmth. "How have you been? How is the world beyond?"

Doris pulled a pack of cigarettes from her pocket and lit one up. She took a deep drag and blew out several perfect smoke rings. "Oh, you know, the usual. Souls living second lives. Souls mourning lost ones. Souls just wanting to forget."

"And how is Jonathan?"

She paused to consider her words. "Incoherent. Inconsolable." She shrugged. "Death is hard, and each soul deals with it differently. You find the ones closest to it are the ones that find it the hardest. Your friend has always walked the line, seeing into the future, remembering too much of the past. He's glimpsed the land of the dead from the corner of his eye and heard its lullaby in his dreams, so being here now is all too real and all too painful. He won't be of any use to you today."

Bane blew out a breath. "He was murdered."

Doris snorted. "We were all murdered. Tell me something unusual."

"The rippers didn't eat him. They just killed him."

Doris stilled. "Oh. Now that *is* new."

If Jonathan couldn't help us right now, maybe she could. Or maybe she could pass on a message. "Do you know who the piper is?"

Doris's lips turned down and she shook

her head. "Can't say I do."

"How long? How long before he's able to speak with us?" Bane asked.

Doris took another drag of her cigarette. "A day, a week, a month? Who knows? Time runs in circles for us. Come back later, whenever that may be, and we will see." She flicked the butt of the cigarette, and it arched through the air and winked out of existence before hitting the ground. "Goodbye, Bane, and good luck."

She turned her back on us and melted into the veil of fireflies.

"Damn it." Bane strode off toward the archway.

"Wait up." I ran to catch up. "We still have all the notebooks from his desk. There must be a clue in there somewhere."

Bane opened the van and grabbed a book from the basket. He flipped it open and held it out. "Can you read this?"

I stared at the words; they were gibberish. "What is that, some kind of code?"

"No. It's some ancient language or other. Jonathan had a passion for dead languages. He made all his notations in them."

Shit. There went my bright idea. We climbed into the van, and Bane had just started the engine when a light bulb switched on in my head. "Oleander."

"What about him?" He slammed the flat of his palm on the dashboard.

"He's an ancient who's been around for a long time."

Bane winced. "Chasing the Hunt. He probably didn't have time to learn dead languages."

"No harm asking?"

Bane fired up the van. "Do it."

Oleander opened his door and peered out into the corridor. His golden hair was mussed and his eyes bloodshot. Had he been crying? My gaze travelled down to note the book in his hand. No, not crying, just reading too much.

I held up the books I'd rescued from the crime scene. "I have a task for you."

Oleander blinked at the leather-bound tomes and then stepped back and opened the door. "Come in, please do."

I strolled into his chambers and bit back a smile. I'd thought Ryker was bad with the bookcases and all the books, but in the short time Oleander had been here he'd managed to transfer half the contents of the library to his room. Books sat in piles up against the wall. They covered his dresser and lay on the floor by his bed in neat piles.

I pressed my lips together to hide a smile. "You know, borrowing a book usually entails returning it."

Oleander grinned sheepishly. "I'm sorry. I

did at first, but then I wanted to re-read the story and had to bring the book back. It's easier to just keep them here."

"Or maybe we could just put a bed in the library for you?"

His eyes lit up. "You could do that?"

I laughed. "No, Oleander. That was a joke."

"Oh." His brow crinkled in confusion. "Aren't jokes meant to be funny?"

Point. "Look, we need your help, Bane and I. A friend of his was murdered."

Oleander's hand flew up to cover his mouth. "Oh, no. Oh, dear."

The image of Jonathan torn and bloody filled my mind's eye. I blinked it away. "It's fine."

He stared at me in horror.

Dammit. "I mean, it's not fine. Just that we're dealing with it fine. He left a note about something or someone called "the piper." We have no idea who that is, but we think there may be a clue in one of these notebooks, but they're written in ancient languages." I flipped one open to show him. "Do you know this language?"

He studied the symbols. "No. But I may be able to decipher it regardless. There are books on linguistics in the library I could use. And I do enjoy a puzzle."

It was better than a kick in the teeth. "Would you mind reading them? Looking for clues on who this piper might be?"

"And that would help the Protectorate."

"Yes, it would."

"More so than cooking meals?"

"Well, the meals are very helpful, but this would also be helpful."

He stood taller. "I would be honored." He took the books from me almost reverently. "I will not disappoint you, Serenity Harker."

Man, he was such a cutie. Sincere and sweet and loyal. How the heck had he messed up and gotten tangled chasing the Wild Hunt for centuries? It was a story he still hadn't told me, not in detail, and it wasn't in me to push him to reveal something that was obviously both embarrassing and painful. He'd been punished enough, and now he was trapped here, in Arcadia, with no way back to the realm of the ancients.

He tucked his hair behind one delicately pointed ear and turned the books over in his hands. "I will start immediately."

"Gosh, no. It's almost midnight. Get some rest, and you can start tomorrow."

Oleander inclined his head.

I left him with the books and the hope that buried somewhere in those pages was a clue as to why Bane's friend had been so brutally killed. In the meantime, Bane was hurting. I'd always thought living a long life was an advantage for nephs, but when Jesse had almost been killed, I'd realized that it was also a curse, especially for those of us who loved a human and who had human friends who'd become family. You got to watch them grow old and die. You got to miss them almost forever. And now Bane was feeling loss.

He'd been there for me when Drayton had been taken; he'd been grieving too, but he'd put his sorrow aside to counsel me and lend me his shoulder.

It was time for me to return the favor.

I found Bane up on the roost. Funny how no one else ever ventured up there, but for me it was like a second home. He'd allowed me into his sanctuary, and yeah, it had been a necessity at the time—daggers under my skin and all that—and though he hadn't needed to allow me back, he had, over and over again. These past six weeks, I'd come up here often just to gaze at the stars, and more often than not he'd been here too.

Tonight, I'd come prepared with a flask of hot chocolate and a packet of his favorite chocolate biscuits. I'd developed a taste for them as well, and just now, in the cupboard, I noted he'd ordered an extra box to accommodate me. Yeah, warm fuzzies over biscuits. I was so soppy.

Bane stood against the balcony with his back to me. "I'm fine, Harker."

I joined him at the ledge. "I'm sure you are,

but since we didn't get to have our meal earlier, I thought I'd bring up some hot chocolate and our favorite biscuits."

"Our favorite?" There was a smile in his voice.

"Thanks for ordering more, by the way."

He shrugged. "I had no choice since *someone* keeps stealing my stash."

His tone was light. Drinks poured, I handed him a cup. He leaned it on the ledge and sighed. "Jonathan was a good person. He didn't deserve to die like that."

I ran a hand down his back, feeling the muscles jump beneath my fingertips. "I'm so sorry, Bane."

He shook his head. "He was old, and age would have taken him soon enough, but he deserved a peaceful end. When I find the person responsible for this, they will know the definition of agony." There was no heat in his words, just a cold finality. He took a long swig of his drink. "This is good. Thank you." He turned to look at me. "You didn't need to do this. I've seen enough death in my time, Harker. I'll be fine. Go get some sleep."

"Well there goes my carefully crafted facade." I passed him the biscuits. "At least eat these."

He flashed me a tired grin that didn't reach his eyes. "Thank you. Just leave them on the bench. I think I'll stretch my wings for a bit."

I stepped back, and he unfurled the matte black bat wings and flexed them, his attention on the stars as if he were already up there among them.

Leaving the flask on the ledge, I headed under the pavilion toward the door.

"Harker?"

I glanced over my shoulder.

"Rain check on that meal."

"Sure."

This time he smiled with his eyes before launching himself up into the air. His wings flapped, once, twice, powerful beats that sent gusts of cold air into my face. And then he was gone, a tiny figure suspended against the creamy moon.

Bane would be okay, but I needed to check on my wounded teammates before I could switch off for the night. The gray stone corridors were silent and spooky this time of night. Every creak, every sigh, was an interruption to the atmosphere of the late hour. Rivers's room was on the other side of the mansion, closest to the roost and farthest from me. I tiptoed into his room, dimly lit by a flickering, rapidly melting candle, and found him on his back, covers pulled up to his chest, fast asleep. Damn, the guy even went to bed in an organized fashion. His soft snores assured me he was alive and well, though. Ha, something he couldn't control.

Orin's room was next, several doors down from mine. He was still stretched out on his mattress, fully clothed and fast asleep, his mouth slightly parted. I carefully tugged off his boots and set them at the foot of the bed, then grabbed the throw scrunched at the bottom of the mattress and pulled it over him. His dark hair was tousled and in his eyes. He seriously needed a trim. Maybe if I asked nicely, he'd let me at his luscious locks with a pair of scissors. My fingers ached to brush back the tendrils, but the last thing I wanted to do was wake him up.

Last stop was Ryker. I entered with a soft click to find him staring at the ceiling wide-eyed and tight-jawed. His bedside lamp bathed him in a muted buttery glow that did nothing to soften the lines of pain etched onto his face.

My chest tightened in alarm. "Oh, hon." I padded over to the bed and gingerly sat by his hip. "The pain's bad, isn't it?"

"I'll be fine. It's not *too* bad. If I could get to sleep, it would speed shit up." He tapped the book lying open on his chest. "I usually read myself to sleep, but I can't focus."

I picked up the book. The title was unfamiliar, but it sounded like a romance novel. Why was I surprised that Ryker, the axe-wielding neph, would be reading this? Oh yeah, because he was Ryker, the axe-wielding neph.

"You want me to read to you?"

He blinked in surprise. "You'd do that?"

I shrugged. "Sure. If it helps."

He held out his arm in invitation for me to lean back against him.

"You sure? What about your stomach?"

"It's fine. Come here." His tone was gruff.

I swung my legs up onto the mattress and settled in the crook of his arm. He adjusted the blanket and draped it over me too. His scent—soap mingled with the coppery smell of blood and man sweat—was a strangely appealing concoction. And could I get any more twisted?

"Chapter fourteen," I read. "The Man and the Rose."

He closed his eyes, and I began to read. I'd reached the end of the chapter when his breathing evened out and his arm around me relaxed. Careful not to jog him, I closed the book and tried to slide out from his embrace. His arm flexed, tightening around me.

Shit. His lips brushed my crown, and a warm sigh fanned the hairs across my forehead. He was finally asleep, and the pain would be muted. It would defeat the purpose of the exercise to risk waking him now. It wasn't like we hadn't slept together before. We'd lain side by side in the cabin during the house games. Sure, this was slightly more intimate, but it was Ryker, and it felt right. Safe. A yawn cracked my jaw. Fuck it.

I closed my eyes and tumbled straight into

a familiar dream.

It was the forest with the lake beyond the trees. A figure appeared to my left. It was me, but not me.

It was my daimon.

"It's almost time," she said.

"Time for what?"

"For the truth to be revealed." She walked toward me. "But I fear we aren't ready."

Wait. Her gaze wasn't on me. She was looking at something over my shoulder. I turned to see a figure, hazy and blurred, standing behind us.

"You are as ready as you'll ever be," the figure said.

This was a voice I recognized. "Ambrosius?"

"Hello, Serenity."

A chill skimmed over my skin. "This isn't a dream, is it?"

"No. It's a warning that will linger and guide you. The veil between our world and theirs thins, and soon the truth will be revealed," Ambrosius said.

"What truth?"

"I do not know. I was to find you, to prepare you and count the days, but I grow weak as the veil thins. My voice does not reach your mind while you are conscious. This may be my only chance to warn you. Your daimon is your anchor."

"I am the anchor," my daimon echoed.

"Keep her fed so she may ground you."

I didn't understand any of this, but … "Okay."

"Your shadow will be your weakness, and when the enemy is released, the truth will be revealed."

He began to fade away.

"Wait!" the daimon called out. "What about the light? Is this about the light?"

But Ambrosius was gone.

I turned to my daimon. "What light?"

She took my hand. "In the lake. I see it in the lake, and I am compelled to shroud it with my darkness. We feed and we protect the light."

"But what is it?"

"I don't know." She reached up to caress my face. "You have kept your word. You have fed me. You have heeded my needs by giving me variety—flavors to satisfy our cravings. I will not fail you."

Maternal warmth surged through me, and tears pricked my eyes. "Did you know our mother? Do you remember?"

Her face twisted in sorrow. "I wish I did not."

Darkness began to close in around us.

"Wait, what does that mean?"

"Serenity, wake up."

Ryker's face hovered above mine. His hair was damp, his torso bare, and he smelled fucking divine.

He laughed and brushed hair off my face. "Hello, sleepy head. Are you there?"

"Mmm." I blinked away the last vestiges of the shadowy dream.

"You kick in your sleep; did you know that? And you mutter and snort."

I grinned and prodded him in the pectoral. "You're lucky I didn't snore."

He sat back. "Oh, you did that too."

I clapped my hands over my face. "Okay, so I'm a messy sleeper."

He stood up and walked over to his wardrobe in his joggers. I propped myself up in bed to find a tray holding coffee and a plate piled high with buttery toast on the bedside table.

God, the coffee smelled good. "Oleander got you breakfast in bed?"

"Nope," Ryker said. "*I* got it for *you.*"

"Me?"

He tugged on a black T-shirt. "As a thank you for reading to me and all the snuggles last night."

My neck heated. "We did not snuggle."

His pupils dilated, eyes darkening, and then he averted his gaze with a nostalgic grin. "Oh, yes, we did. Now eat up. The humans arrive in less than an hour, and you need to get the training room ready."

"Seeing as you seem to have healed, fancy

helping out?"

"I need another few hours before I'm up to combat, even sparring. I checked the rota and we're on patrol together later, and I want to be a hundred percent by then."

"Fine. I'll let you off this time. But you're helping tomorrow."

"You can count on it." He grabbed a slice of toast off the tray. "Now, eat your breakfast before I change my mind and claim it for myself."

Ava lay on her back on the mat, her eyes glazed. Oh, shit. I'd hit her too hard.

"Damn, Ava. I'm so sorry."

She shook her head and rolled onto her side. Her shoulders began to shake. We'd been going at this for the past two hours, sparring and tumbling and climbing the apparatus and leaping. She was good—athletic and determined—and for a moment, I'd forgotten she was only human, and now she was broken.

She rolled onto her back, her face creased in laughter. Oh, thank God. "Get up, idiot. You had me worried."

She took my hand and allowed me to haul her up, and then she doubled over to catch her breath.

"You want to call it a day?"

Around us, the other members of her unit were in various stages of training. Some were sparring with members of the Protectorate, and others were running the obstacle course while being timed by Bane. His voice was a boom as he bellowed taunts and encouragement in equal measure. There was no going easy on this lot if we wanted them up to scratch.

Ava held up her hand. "No stopping. We continue. We've got just over two weeks before the scourge run, and I aim to get signed off by then." She glanced in Bane's direction. "At least he's taking us seriously now."

I followed her gaze, lingering on Bane's harsh profile. He'd pulled back his hair from his forehead and tied it in a man bun, and damn, he looked fucking hot. I blinked and shook off the errant totally inappropriate thought, but a gnawing flared to life in the pit of my stomach.

Feed. My daimon's voice filled my mind. Yeah, I needed to get on that, but not with Bane, no matter how much I wanted to feel that honey power coursing through my veins.

"We all realize how important this is for Midnight. Things are getting worse out there, and we need you guys."

She nodded curtly. "So, let's continue. Teach me."

"All right, let's go another round."

We fell into fighting stance again. It was hand-to-hand this week, and next week we'd move on to weapons. The humans preferred guns to blades and swords, but guns ran out of ammo, so they needed to learn how to wield a blade as backup. My body went into autopilot mode, moving on instinct and holding back enough so as not to hurt Ava too much, but that was nothing new for me. I'd held back all the time in Sunset. Training with the humans was kinda like coming home.

We finished up with Ava pinned to the mat. She tapped out to say she was done. A shadow fell over us, and I looked up to find Bane standing over us.

"You need to feed," he said shortly.

Great, announce it to the world, why don't you? And how the heck did he always seem to know. I released Ava and stood up. "I'm fine for a bit longer."

"Now, Harker."

His tone grated, and the urge to snap back, to argue, was a physical pressure in my head, but to do that would be to undermine the chain of command—something we were going to be drumming into the human unit over the next couple of weeks. Back-chatting Bane would be bad role modelling.

"Yes, sir." There was no harm in a mock salute, though.

Bane snorted. "Kim, come here." He gestured to a young female neph who'd been watching from the sidelines. "Keep Ava here warm for a bit."

He gently gripped my elbow and steered me from the room. I tore my arm from his grasp as soon as we got outside.

"What the fucking hell was that?"

He frowned. "You need to feed."

"Yeah. I know that, and I will in my own time. You didn't have to make an issue out of it in there."

Bane's eyes narrowed. "You reek of need. You reek of desire. I can barely concentrate in there because of the vibes coming off you." He moved closer, trapping me up against the wall. "Feed now before—"

"Before what?"

"Before I fuck you."

The breath slammed out of my lungs. "You can't ... you can't say that. Don't." Damn my breathy voice.

My daimon purred.

He inhaled deeply then leaned in to run the tip of his nose up my cheek. "Harker, let's fuck."

Heat exploded low in my belly and my heart did a back flip. Oh, man. Oh, God. I wanted ... so bad ... but it would cross a line and take me somewhere I wasn't emotionally ready to go. Sex, for me, was tied with emotion, not just the hunger, and that was a part of me that was still raw and vulnerable. Drayton had been safe—an incubus used to the courtship dance—and we'd both known there was never to be a culmination, but we'd played along, pretending in our bubble for a little while. But Bane … if I let him touch me, let him inside, then I'd be lost, because for me it would be more than sex, and for him … I just didn't know. My body was screaming at me to step into him, to touch, feel, caress, but I remained absolutely still.

"No."

He pulled away and then stepped back. "Then feed." He held out his arm.

I couldn't. Not off him, not now while my pulse was racing and my body was aching for him. "You should get back in there and supervise. I'll ask Orin."

His expression shuttered. "Fine. Be quick."

He strode off, seemingly unaffected by the moment of closeness we'd shared, but it was a good minute before my body was able to peel itself from the wall and stand upright.

By the time I found Orin in the kitchen, my body was trembling with need. He was leaning up against the counter chatting amiably to Oleander when I barged in.

They broke off their conversation as I entered.

Orin turned to me with a smile. "Hey, how are—"

I grabbed his shirt and pulled him against me. "I need to feed." The voice wasn't mine, it was the daimon's, deep and throaty and hungry.

Orin's eyes widened, his mouth parted.

"Orin, do I have your consent?" Dammit, I needed it now.

He nodded. Usually, I'd make do with skin on skin contact, my hands on his chest or his arms, but not today. Today, I needed more. I needed lips and tongue and the clash of teeth. Orin let out a yelp as I grabbed the back of his neck and pulled him down. My lips slanted across his, demanding entrance. His body tensed and then his mouth parted, allowing me entry, and his arms closed around me, drawing me close. Yes. Damn, he felt good, hard and taut in all the right places, as I leaned in to him so my breasts were squashed against his chest and my leg was hooked around his thigh. Strawberries — he tasted of strawberries. The slide of his tongue against mine was a heady rush that shot straight to my core.

Feed.

Oh, yeah. I began to draw power, green and tangy with a briny finish that reminded me of the sea. It coursed into me, steady and solid and secure. Orin's fingers tangled in my hair, massaging my scalp and sending delicious tingles through me. Through my rapidly satiating hunger came the awareness that he held me lightly, as if I were made of glass and could shatter at the slightest pressure. He held me like a man would hold a precious lover.

My consciousness surfaced, pushing past the clawing need and slamming into the driver's seat. I tore my mouth from his, but he remained still, eyes closed, luscious lashes fanning against his cheeks. His heart beat hard and fast against the palm of my hand.

"Thank you." My voice was a whisper.

His eyelids fluttered open, trapping me in stormy seas. "My pleasure," he said in a low, breathless rumble.

He didn't release me, though, his light touch holding me captive. My scalp prickled a moment before Orin's attention shifted over my head. His dreamy expression melted into a cross between sorrow and guilt. I glanced over my shoulder to find Cassie standing in the doorway, her face expressionless. How had she gotten past the sentinels?

I stepped out of Orin's embrace and crossed my arms. "Come to clear out your room?"

She blinked and then swallowed, tearing her gaze from Orin. "I came to get my job back, actually. To come and make amends, but I see now that it's too late to make some things right." Her lips curled in a self-deprecating smile. "I guess I deserve it."

It was obvious she thought Orin and I were a thing, and I was half-tempted to let her believe it. She deserved worse for what she'd done to him, but lies had a way of getting convoluted.

I opened my mouth to set her straight, but Orin's arm slid around my waist, cutting off my words.

He yanked me to him and rested his chin on the top of my head. "You'd best find Bane, then. I believe he's in the training room with the humans."

Did he just press a kiss to the top of my head?

Cassie blanched, spun on her heel, and clambered up the steps.

"Well …" Oleander picked up a tray laden with a pot of tea and a plate of biscuits. "Things certainly never get dull around here." He walked toward the door. "I will inform you once I have deciphered the notebooks." He threw the words over his shoulder on the way out.

I rounded on Orin. "What was that?"

He touched his bottom lip with his index finger. "A kiss?"

I sighed. "Orin, you have to tell her."

"No. I don't. It's not my problem if she jumps to conclusions. It's not my problem if she hurts."

The last was said with less conviction.

I pressed a hand to his chest. "You don't mean that, because that isn't who you are." I tilted my chin to look into his gentle face. "You're a good man, Orin. A kind, loyal man. Don't let her take that away from you."

He cupped my face and pressed a kiss to

the tip of my nose. "Damn you, Harker," he said softly.

Why did I get the impression he was talking about more than Cassie? This was about the kiss. "I'm sorry I kissed you."

He winced. "Ouch."

Shit. "I mean, I shouldn't have taken advantage like that."

His expression sobered. "We're a team. We work as a unit. A weak link brings us all down, so if you need to feed, you feed, any way you need to. You're cambion and the hunger is part of you. It makes you who you are. There's no need to apologize. I'm here for you. We all are."

Except Ryker. Ryker still hadn't offered to let me siphon off him, and to be honest, I wasn't too keen on getting that close with an empath. Having my emotions and deepest desires on display was not appealing, especially when there was so much I didn't understand myself.

"What are you going to do about Cassie?"

"Nothing." He smiled sadly. "Cassie and I are over. If Bane lets her come back, then she'll be a part of the team and nothing else." His smile turned teasing. "You can stop worrying about me."

"Fine, but only if you make some more scones later."

"Deal."

The post-kiss moment was defused, but as I clambered up the steps to the main floor it hit me that it hadn't been awkward. Not at all.

"He let me back in."

I glanced up from zipping up my boots to see Cassie leaning up against my bedroom doorway.

A spike of annoyance cut through me, but I schooled my face into nonchalance. "Good for you."

She sighed. "Look. I just wanted to say I'm sorry for being such a bitch the past few weeks. I got caught up in my own shit, and I let you all down. I just want a second chance and a fresh start. Do you think we can do that?"

Oh, man. She sounded and looked sincere, but then why was my gut pricking in warning?

"Harker, I really hope we can be friends." She pushed off the frame and walked away.

I grabbed my jacket off my bed. Everyone deserved a second chance, right? Maybe it was time to just let it go. If Bane had let her come back, then he must believe she deserved to be here, and even though my boss was a gruff, arrogant pain in the ass, his judgment was always spot-on. Still, it rankled that he'd let her back so quickly.

It was almost time for patrol, and Ryker would be waiting in the foyer for me. I was in the mood for some real combat action.

It was quiet. Way too quiet. The lull before the storm, that's what it was, and Ryker and I had spent the whole of patrol feeling antsy and shifty. It was with relief we entered the Protectorate mansion. It had been the same for the past couple of weeks. Since Cassie had rejoined the crew, in fact. Not that there was any correlation, just ... it hardly seemed fair that she got to put her feet up as soon as Bane took her back.

Oleander, Rivers, and Orin were ensconced in the lounge. Rivers and Orin were hunched over a chess board, and Oleander was curled up in the wingback with a book. One of Jonathan's notebooks. A notepad lay on his lap, and his face was scrunched up in concentration as he scanned the pages.

He looked up absently as I parked myself beside Rivers.

"This man, Jonathan, was amazing," he

said. "He was researching the wards around the city. Looking into boundary spells and their origins."

"What about this piper he mentioned?"

He shrugged. "No mention yet, but I still have three notebooks to go through. This one is written in Sumerian."

No clue what that was. Thank God we had Oleander on our team. My feet throbbed dully in my boots. All the training, walking, and the general being on my feet for the past two weeks were finally catching up. But there would be no rest, because the scourge was due to run tomorrow.

I raised a boot. "Damn, my feet ache." I leaned back against the sofa. "Where's the boss?"

Rivers swung my legs into his lap and then pulled off my boots.

"Nooo!" Orin held up his hands. "Not the sweaty feet."

"It's fine." I tried to tug my feet from Rivers's grasp. "I'm fine."

"No. You're not. We've all seen how hard you've worked to get the humans ready for tomorrow. The scourge is going to run, and thanks to your stubbornness, we'll have fifteen more boots on the ground with us." He said it matter-of-factly.

No way, he was not going to … foot massage. I melted into the sofa. His hands were firm, sure, practiced. Damn, Rivers had some skills.

"You know what, your shoulders look tense too," Orin said. His tone was serious, but his eyes twinkled with mischief.

He left his seat and slipped in beside me on the four seater. His strong hands settled on my neck and shoulders, and he began to knead the knotted muscles into submission.

Oh fucking hell, that felt amazing.

"I suppose I should make madam a cup of tea?" Oleander said from his spot on the wingback.

Ryker snorted. "Hey, I've been out too. How come I don't get a massage?"

"Come here." I waved him over and indicated he sit on the floor by my hip.

He moved so fast, he was almost a blur. Orin choked back a laugh as I began to massage Ryker's scalp. He leaned his head back against me and closed his eyes. His golden tresses slipped through my fingers, and Ryker leaned into my touch.

For a moment, it was just the five of us cocooned in comfortable companionship. This was home. The only person missing from the picture was Bane.

"Well, isn't this cozy," Cassie said as she strolled in. She walked up to the drinks trolley and poured herself a generous measure of scotch. "But shouldn't you guys get a room?"

Orin's hands stilled. Anger surged up inside me at the implication, at the fact that she was turning something innocent and loving into something sexual and sordid. My retort was still forming on my tongue when Rivers beat me to it.

"Not everything is about sex, Cassie," he said. "There are other relationships between a male and female."

She tossed back her drink. "Yeah? Like friends with benefits. Or where one party has the hots for the other and the other is clueless and totally in the friend zone. Or like when every guy in the room looks for a reason to touch or be touched by a particular female because anything is better than nothing." Her lip curled in a sneer.

Who was this person? And where was the Cassie who'd apologized to me less than two weeks ago?

Cassie poured another drink, tongue flicking out to tease the corner of her mouth as a wicked gleam entered her eyes. "When all the time the true object of said female's sexual obsession is about to get fucked by someone else."

My pulse skipped, and Rivers's hands tensed on my feet. My gaze flew to his face. Wait. Had this been some kind of distraction?

Rivers sighed and closed his eyes. "He didn't want you to know."

I was off the sofa and out the door in a

heartbeat.

There was no standing on ceremony this time, no knocking, no waiting. I barged into Bane's bedchamber, heart in my mouth, to find him standing at the foot of the bed, his torso bare, while a lingerie-clad Lilith stood before him, her crimson-tipped fingers on his pectorals.

His expressionless face twisted into one of anger at my interruption, but the glint in his eyes was all shame.

"Get away from him." My voice was a menacing hiss. "Get your fucking hands off him, now."

"Harker, what the fuck?" Bane snapped.

Lilith held up a hand and slowly turned to face me. Her scarlet lips curled in a thin smile, and her dark eyes narrowed. "You presume to give me orders?"

Adrenaline coursed through my veins, hot and potent, and in that moment, I didn't give a shit who she was or what she might do to me. The snap and crackle in the air served only to heighten my rage, and I took a threatening step toward her.

"I'll do more than fucking presume if you don't get your skinny arse out of here now."

Her left eye twitched. "Oh, really?"

She threw out an arm, and the air itself slammed into me, propelling me across the room into the wall. My head cracked against brick, and stars bloomed in my vision. Bane's voice was a brutal bellow pulling me out of the arms of impending unconsciousness, dragging me back to my feet and straight at a wide-eyed Lilith. I slammed into her, taking her down. It was my turn to slam her head on the floor, and then I was being hauled off her by a muscled forearm.

"Enough. Damn it, Harker," Bane ordered.

He held me tight while I kicked and thrashed, the thought of her with him drilling holes in my brain.

He spun me round to face him and gripped my wrists with one hand. "Stop." His voice was a sharp slap.

I stilled, staring up into his proud face, into those depthless eyes filled with regret. My breath hitched and my eyes welled. "I can't."

Laughter rippled in the air behind us — real, bubbling, unstoppable laughter. Bane's gaze slipped from my face to the manically giggling figure on the floor.

"Lilith?" He released me and held out a hand to her.

She waved him away with her hand. "Oh, goodness. Oh, my. It's been a long time since anyone challenged me like that." She shook her head and wiped at her eyes. "To think there was a time when I was revered and feared." She exhaled and sobered. "To think there was a time when people trembled at my name." She pulled herself to her feet and adjusted her negligee. "We have a deal, Bane. A contract." She looked to me and shrugged. "I will have my quota of sexual energy one way or the other."

One way or the other? "Then we'll make it the other."

She arched a brow and smiled. "I want sexual energy born from sex, little cambion. This time nothing else will do."

Don't think about it, don't worry about the implications, my daimon whispered. *We can't let her have him.* "Fine. You have a deal. Now, please, get out."

Beside me, Bane had gone completely still. Lilith inclined her head and then grabbed her robe and swept from the room.

I slumped against the bed.

"Harker, what did you do?"

I turned to him, my heartbeat a jackrabbit in my chest. "Gave us an excuse to take what we both want."

His eyes flared. "Serenity."

"I won't have her touch you. Ever again. I can't."

He took a step toward me. "I'll hurt you. I'm not a gentle lover."

I reached up to graze his cheek with my fingertips. "I can take it."

A low growl reverberated inside his chest, and this time when he swept me off my feet, I didn't fight him. He flung me onto the bed, my head bounced off the mattress, and my teeth caught my lip. My tongue flicked out to soothe it, and the coppery taste of blood pricked my senses. And then he was climbing up onto the mattress. His huge body hovered over me, and his scent — fresh and sweet and sharp — filled my head as his thick thighs bracketed mine.

"We'll do this on the mattress this time because it's the first time." His tone was rough, like calluses caressing my sensitized senses.

The first time, because there would be more — there'd have to be to feed Lilith. My mind rationalized even though my insides were turning molten at the sight of him above me.

"Why? Where would we do it otherwise?" My voice came out breathless and raspy.

He leaned in to dip his nose into the crook of my neck and inhaled. "The floor, or up against the wall." His tongue flicked out to taste me. "The window seat, or maybe the shower." His fangs grazed my carotid, and my heart stuttered as my back arched involuntarily. "We could take a run, and I could fuck you up against the cold marble pillars in the ruins."

Each word was a caress, priming me, softening me, and tightening me all at the same time. My pulse was a trapped bird in my throat. And when his powerful hands closed around my thighs, a moan tore from my lips, surprising me with the wantonness of it.

He pried my legs apart and then cupped me through the fabric of my slacks. "This is mine," he said, and then he tore the damn slacks off my body, leaving me exposed in my pink lace panties. Cold air slicked across my throbbing flesh. His mouth parted, and his chest heaved. "Mine." He ripped the delicate fabric, the sound like liberation, and buried his head between my thighs.

My breath exploded as his tongue found me, hot and determined. He latched on with his mouth and began to play me. There was nothing but the heat of his lips, the lapping of his tongue, and the bolts of lightning that shot through my body, forcing it to buck, and tense, and contort. Hands in his hair, silken between my fingers, scalp against my nails. The pressure built, tightening, almost painfully. The air was heavy, thick with power and sexual energy, red and blue and gold. He was going to make me —oh, fuck. I threw my head back and abandoned myself to the throb and pulse of my sex as he devoured my orgasm. Blood roared in my ears, and my limbs quivered with the aftershocks. No more, fucking hell. That tongue …

I needed his mouth on mine. I fisted his hair and yanked him up my body, finding his lips and tasting myself on them. His flesh was taut and velvet beneath my fingers as I clawed at his back, his shoulders. He settled against me, cradled between my thighs, his weight pressing me into the bed, his hardness lying like steel against me. But there was fabric. His fucking bottoms. They needed to go. I needed to feel him sliding and teasing against my swollen sex. One hand between us to free him and then a shift of the hips would do it. Just a nudge and I'd have him inside me. I reached for him but never made it. His fingers bit into my wrists as he held my hands immobile over my head with one powerful hand. His grip was uncompromising, brutal, and painful. Yes, this would bruise, but fuck, it felt good. He reared up and grabbed the neck of my shirt and pulled downward. The fabric ripped, and air kissed my skin, whisper-soft and cool against my fevered flesh. My nipples puckered instantly, hard and straining for his lips and teeth. He obliged with the scrape of incisors and the stab of fang against the sensitized nubs tightening and begging for more. He covered them in heat, licking, sucking, and drawing on them until the sensation inside me was a coiled spring ready to snap.

Now. My daimon began to feed, to take from him. Honey power slid into my veins. Climbing from my toes, up my legs, and settling at my core as the energy built. *Now. We need him now.*

I bucked, trying to free my hands, wanting to touch him, wanting to—his mouth captured mine, his tongue thrusting between my lips, silencing my protests with a blast of power to hold me immobile. It was in my head—an expanding supernova of pleasure that numbed the bite of his fingers on my thighs as he forced them wider. He yanked me toward him, angling my hips. Somewhere in the periphery of awareness the realization that my hands were now free flitted along the edges of my consciousness. But nothing mattered but his violet eyes, the erratic rise and fall of his mammoth chest. He hooked a thumb into his pants and slowly, deliberately slid them down, freeing himself—bronzed and hard and fucking huge. A guttural moan of need filled the air. Me, that was me. His eyes lit up, and he splayed a hand over my abdomen, the tips of his fingers grazing my breasts.

"Don't fucking move." His voice was a deep rumble. An order.

I nodded. Eyes on the prize. Nothing mattered but his manhood pressing against me. Nothing mattered but the push and slide of desire.

"Please." Was that me whimpering?

He entered me on a single thrust, tearing a cry from my lips, equal parts pleasure and pain, and then he began to move and the pain was overshadowed by a sweet, electric sensation. His power rammed into me with each thrust, filling me, invading me, pushing me to the edge of an abyss.

"Serenity. Fucking hell."

My turn. The daimon took over, spilling her strength into my limbs, and together we took him down, pinning him beneath us, taking him deeper with each roll of our hips. Bane threw back his head, letting out a guttural cry that reverberated between us.

Deeper, faster, harder.

And then I was no longer in control. I was pinned against the headboard, his hand tangled in my hair, my head yanked so far back a stab of pure terror cut through me. Yeah, he could break my neck, just snap it like a twig, but then his tongue was in my mouth, mimicking his thrusts, and there was no more thought.

There was only the sex, and the power.

There was only Bane.

We lay side by side, the glow of sexual energy wreathing us like heady incense. The back of our hands brushed and our breath came shallow and fast.

"That was ... wow." I closed my eyes and licked my lips, savoring the aftershocks still rippling through my body.

"Let's hope we haven't scarred Ambrosius for life," Bane said.

I let out a short bark of laughter. "No. I don't think he's here. I haven't heard from him in weeks." A niggle at the back of my mind. "I think ... I think I may have dreamed of him, though. Yes, I think I did."

He rolled onto his side. "What happened?"

The dream was fuzzy and far away, but the sense of importance and urgency came back to me now. "I think he was trying to warn me about something." Dammit. What was it?

The veil is thinning and all will be revealed when the enemy is released, my daimon said.

I looked up into his harsh face and resisted the urge to run my fingers across his stubble. "Something about a veil thinning."

He frowned. "Could he be talking about the barrier around Arcadia?"

"I don't know. Possibly."

"No point in worrying until we have more information."

He was right, of course. We had more pressing matters, like the scourge run tomorrow, and passing Lilith this power, and figuring out where this thing we had was going? I was suddenly very aware of how naked and exposed I was and how the cool air clung to the perspiration on my skin.

"It doesn't have to mean anything," Bane said softly.

I met his gaze. "I know, but I think it already does. We just need to figure out what it is."

The corner of his mouth lifted in a smirk. "There's only one way to do that."

Cheeky bugger. I gave him my best

innocent expression. "Take a personality quiz from one of those magazines?"

His pupils dilated. "No. We can fuck more."

I exhaled sharply. Damn him and his solar plexus-punching words. Bane didn't play games. He didn't skirt issues. He got to the crux of a matter, he got what he wanted, and he got in deep. And I really needed to stop thinking in these metaphors, because, was it hot in here?

"I should go pay Lilith." I swung my legs off the bed, then realized my clothes were in shreds. "Um … do you have a robe I can borrow?"

"Back of the bathroom door."

His attention was a hot brand on my skin all the way to the bathroom. The robe was huge, falling to my ankles and completely swamping me. It smelled of Bane. Sweet yet masculine, just like his power.

I padded back into the bedroom. "What did you get out of the deal?"

He propped himself up on his elbow, muscles rippling beneath velvet skin, abs crunching. His hair had come loose from his tie, and it framed his harsh face becomingly. "I can't remember."

"What?"

He swallowed hard. "It is my blood, my signature on the contract, my power, and my scent, and yet I can't recall why I signed it. There is nothing in it to give me a clue as to what I got from the deal."

"But that's crazy."

He climbed off the bed and walked over to me; fuck, he was getting hard again. And what had we just been talking about?

He undid the tie on the robe and slid his hot hands beneath to cup my hips. "What's crazy is how fuckable you look in my robe."

He was trying to distract me. "Bane, seriously, why hasn't she told you?"

He sighed and released me. "She says she is under oath not to."

"And you believe her?"

"Yes, I do." He strode over to the foot of the bed and picked up his pants and pulled them on. "Let's go and give her what she wants."

"I'll do it." I walked to the door. "I'd rather do it alone."

For a moment it looked like he'd argue, but then he nodded curtly. "If that's what you want."

"It is."

Leaving him to dress, I set out to find the succubus.

Lilith stood warming her skanky ass by the hearth in the lounge. The others had obviously made themselves scarce, not that she seemed to mind. Drink in hand, she looked perfectly at ease.

Her brows flicked up as I walked toward her. "Nice robe," she said.

"Put the glass down, and let's get this over with."

The thought of putting my mouth on hers made my skin crawl, but this was sexual energy, and instinct told me it was the only way to transfer it. It swelled inside me, as if indignant at the prospect of being expelled.

Lilith set her glass on the mantel and puckered up.

Urgh. I planted one on her and released the energy I'd collected. At first it clung to me, reluctant to go. Come on, daimon, a little help here? A chuckle and then the power flooded out of me and into Lilith. The succubus was practically vibrating with joy. And then the flow cut off, prematurely. My daimon was doing a sneaky and holding a little back, but fair play, we'd done all the work, right?

Lilith staggered back. "Now that is a hit worth waiting for." Her tone was thick and satisfied. "Can I assume this new arrangement stands for future collections?"

"Yeah. You not touching Bane works fine with us both."

She studied me for a long beat. "Be careful, little cambion. Do not forget what you are. Bane's power is heady and seductive, but it will never be enough for you."

"If I need advice, I'll ask."

Her smile fell away. "No, you won't. You're too stubborn for that, but I'm feeling magnanimous so I'm going to give you some pearls of wisdom free of charge."

"Whoop-de-doo."

She ignored me and continued. "For a succubus, sexual energy is a meal just like any other, and variety is essential to moral well-being. It's the same for a cambion. One flavor of power will never be enough. But you know that already, don't you?"

My throat tightened. "I don't know what you mean."

She threw back her head and laughed. "Don't ever play poker, girl. You don't have the face for it. You've been siphoning off the Protectorate males, haven't you?"

"What if I have?"

She shrugged. "Nothing. Just making a point."

"I just don't want to rely on one person, that's all. It wouldn't be fair."

"To who? Them or you?"

"Them, of course." But the words sounded hollow, even to me. They tasted of lies, because yeah, the variety, the *flavor*, as she called it, was intoxicating. Orin was a serene sea, balmy ocean, fresh and relaxing. Rivers was an electric storm, sharp and dangerous and invigorating, and Bane was my hot spring, the honey that soothed every ache and pain and recharged me.

"You know I'm right. You know what you need, what you crave, and where there is craving, there is desire." She took a step closer. "You may not *need* sexual energy to survive, but you will *want* it, and just like any meal, you will need a variety of it."

"You don't know anything about me. I don't fuck around. Sex is emotional for me, not just physical."

"And you think you can only have that with one person?"

What was she implying?

"Feeding opens a visceral connection, one rooted in rutting and carnal desire. We are carnal beings, and there is nothing to be ashamed of. You may have accepted your daimon, but you still haven't handed over the reins and allowed her to show you what you truly are. You won't be complete until you do."

"I believe in soul mates."

She laughed. "Your daimon *is* your soul mate, haven't you realized that by now?"

No, I hadn't, but she didn't need to know that. She didn't need to have the last word. "I've managed fine on just power so far. But thanks for the insight."

"Of course you have. And you've wondered, in the throes of a feeding, what it would be like to take it further than skin on skin.

What it would be like to feed with lips and tongue. You've done it now. You've tasted sexual energy and been forced to give it up to me. Now, what would it be like to keep it for yourself?"

My pulse kicked up at the thought, at the memory of Orin's mouth on mine, his hand caressing my scalp. I tamped down on it. The bitch would not rile me up.

"We are done." I turned on my heel and strode out of the room, which would have gone better if the damned robe hadn't tripped me up.

Her laughter followed me up the stairs.

None of us could bear cleaning out Drayton's room, and for some reason, my feet took me there now. Standing in the doorway, I scanned his personal space. The bed was still unmade. His chess game still in play. An ironed shirt that would never be worn hung on the back of the wardrobe, and his hairbrush lay on the dresser, carrying strands of his hair. I padded over to the bed and perched on the edge of the mattress. The sheets still smelled of him, and the scent went straight to my heart, coaxing a deep ache that would probably never heal. I held his pillow to my face and inhaled deeply. My eyes burned and pricked.

"I miss him too," Bane said from the doorway.

I held out the pillow. "You want to sniff?"

He smiled wanly. "I can smell him from here."

"Oh, yeah, with your super senses."

He wandered over to the bed and sat beside me. The mattress dipped, pushing me against him.

He slung an arm about my shoulders and pulled me close. "The Protectorate is a team, and when I took on the role of boss it meant there had to be some distance between me and the others. They needed to respect that boundary, but Dray"—he chuckled—"Dray didn't do boundaries. He got in my face about everything all the time. He was impossible to stay pissed at and impossible not to love. He was my closest friend."

My chest grew hollow at the pain in his words. "I knew you guys were close, but ..."

He sighed. "I'd sacrifice anything to have him back." He turned to look at me. "Even if it meant losing whatever we've begun to cultivate."

His violet eyes were dark with sorrow and regret, as if it were already coming to pass. As if Drayton had walked back into our lives, and this, this thing we'd started, was over. But it wouldn't be over. It couldn't.

Lilith's words echoed in my ears, and I pushed them away, reaching up to caress the stubble along his jaw. "I don't think even

Drayton coming back could change the way I feel about you."

His breath caught, and his throat bobbed. The mighty Bane, thrown and unsure? I'd done this with a mere sentence, and damn, that was intoxicating.

"And how *do* you feel about me?" he pressed.

My emotions were a cocktail of need, and desire, and protectiveness. This thing with Bane was like untangling an intricate knot on a beautifully wrapped gift. I wouldn't know what was inside until I worked it through. "I'm not sure yet, but I'd like the chance to find out." I caught my bottom lip between my teeth and slowly released it, triumphant when his gaze settled on my mouth and his breathing grew shallow. "Maybe we could start with a shower?"

His lips parted in a smile that revealed his fangs, sending a delicious tremor of anticipation shooting up my spine.

"I think that can be arranged."

7

Ava and the human unit covered sector two, linked to us via comms and ready to receive the signal flare once we knew what direction the scourge was coming from. Bane had made it clear that if they were going to participate in the scourge run then they needed to act as an extension of the MPD. Any other time, they could refer to their own chain of command. We'd allocated sectors for regular patrol, but the scourge was an unpredictable beast, and to tame it, we needed to work together as a single unit.

Orin and Rivers were parked on a rooftop with me while we waited for action. Bane, Ryker, and Cassie made up the other team, and the other Protectorates had been split into teams of four. With the humans on board, we had more than enough eyes on the street. My hands itched to release the daggers, and my daimon settled back for the show. This was all me. She'd done her part earlier when we'd fed from Rivers, and now my body crackled with his electric energy.

The flare went up in the east. Sector two, where the humans were. We burst into action, running along the rooftops, sliding down pipes, climbing up steps, and then doing it all over again. Orin and Rivers were shadows at my back and by my side. We kept together, moving like the wind, and then a flare went up to the west.

Fuck!

"Bane, what do you want us to do?"

"Misfire. Ignore. Continue east, we're on our way."

Thank goodness the scourge was playing by the rules, but then why was my gut doing crazy somersaults?

Sector two loomed up ahead, but the noise of battle reached us way before we passed the invisible borders into the territory—the putter of gunfire, the growl and roar of the rippers, the swipe of blades cutting through the air, and the screams of those that didn't make it. We staggered to a halt at the edge of a flat roof. It was the corner of an industrial estate. It made no sense. There were no humans here, aside from Ava and her unit. Why would the scourge attack here, unless …

"It's a fucking trap." Bane's voice crackled in our ears.

"Where are you?" I glanced about.

"Three o'clock."

There he was, hurtling through an alley

right into the action. Protectorate and humans swung swords and firearms against the claw and fang of the rippers as they tried desperately to break through the circle of scourge that had them penned in.

"They lured us here. They want to take us down in force," Bane yelled.

And there were too many of them, all focused on killing us. They didn't give a shit about feeding tonight. Tonight was about us.

"Harker, get the guys and get out of here. Abort. Do you hear me?" Bane ordered.

Ryker was down there too, but there was no sign of Cassie. Below us, Bane swung into action, taking out four rippers with one sweep of his mammoth sword. There was no going back, no aborting for the units on the ground.

I turned to Orin and Rivers. "I can't."

Orin nodded. "We're not going anywhere. We're in this together. I'll watch your back, Rivers will watch mine, and you keep an eye on Rivers. Got it?"

"Got it," Rivers and I said in unison, and then we were scaling the building and hitting the ground running.

Blood and carnage and rage, so much rage, emanating off these creatures. Vengeance was the only hunger here. As my blades did their work and my daimon channeled power into my limbs, I couldn't help but wonder what the fuck they wanted vengeance for? How had the mindless beasts suddenly begun planning coups and setting traps?

What the heck was going on?

"The Breed!" Bane's voice was a boom in my ear.

Whoops and howls filled the air as The Breed leapt down toward us from the surrounding buildings—ten, twenty, thirty, more. Shit, we were so screwed.

But then a wave of rippers began to retreat. The rest held their ground, flanked by suckers.

"Rivers, take Ava's unit and follow the rippers," Bane ordered. "The rest of you, stand your ground."

The Breed and scourge were working together! The scourge had lured us here so The Breed could take us out. It was no longer claws against blade. It was blade on blade, because The Breed had come armed. We were outnumbered two to one, and all I could think about was finding Maximilian and making him pay. As humans followed Rivers and Ava in cutting a swathe through the carnage in pursuit of the retreating rippers, Orin and I set to work on The Breed.

Time stopped as we fought, side by side, back to back. The *clang* and *chink* of metal on metal, the *whoosh* and slice of blades as they cut through the night air, was a symphony of combat. But we were losing. Protectorate were cut down in the periphery of my vision by the larger, more powerful Breed males. It was only a matter of time before we were overwhelmed.

We fought on with aching arms and blood-spattered limbs, our voices raw from battle cries. A new timbre of howl cut through the chaos. Lower, ominous, and familiar to my ears. My pulse quickened. It couldn't be, could it?

"Lupin in the fray!" Bane's voice echoed through my ear piece.

I caught a glimpse of Gregory, the Lupin leader, to my right, his teeth bared as he slashed at a ripper with his lethal claws.

"Harker, watch out!" Orin yelled.

I jumped back, and a ripper sailed past me, its jaws ready to snap, its eyes on a prize that wasn't me. I spun in time to see it grab one of the human males who hadn't made it out with Rivers. Its jaws clamped on the human's arm and swept him off his feet. The human's scream was like glass shards digging into my brain, and then he was dragged into the gaping maw of one of the many buildings dotting the estate.

My gut screamed that Max was out here somewhere, and the desire for vengeance battled my moral code.

Damn it!

Darkness enveloped me, cutting off the light of the moon as I dove into the building after the ripper and its prey. Down a corridor and through a set of double doors that swung onto what must have been, at some point, a factory floor. It was abandoned and empty now except for the ripper, the human, and … Cassie?

Thank God. She'd save the human.

Cassie lowered her blade and stepped back, and the ripper tore out the human's throat. A scream bubbled up from mine. Cassie's body tensed, and she turned to face me. The ripper raised its head to look at me too, and there it was, clear as day in both their eyes—death, darkness, and an endless abyss of nothingness.

My stomach clenched in horror. This was not Cassie. "Who are you?"

The thing wearing Cassie's face smiled. And then she lunged, bridging the gap between us in a blur. There was only her face, so close, so terrifyingly beautiful and alien, smiling reassuringly.

"Consider this a blessing," she said.

She looked down, and I followed her gaze to find her blade buried in my abdomen all the way to the hilt. All the way. Pain bloomed, fire and ice, sharp and sudden, robbing me of breath.

Bootfalls echoed off the walls, distant but approaching fast. My limbs were frozen. My mouth was open in an 'o' of surprise.

Cassie pulled the blade out, her expression shuttering.

"Harker!"

Cassie was knocked off her feet by a whirlwind of muscle, but the world was fading into a sea of pain, and my knees could no longer hold me up.

No, this cannot be. No. Serenity, hold on to life. Hold on to your anchor.

Ambrosius, you bastard. Where have you been? Look, I got stabbed, but you know that, don't you? My words filled my head but refused to spill from my lips.

I have you. My daimon channeled energy into me; every ounce of power we had left filled my limbs, but my life force was seeping out too fast.

"Ryker! Do something," Rivers demanded. Was he sobbing? Why was he crying?

Familiar arms circled me, lifting me up and infusing me with heat and surrounding me with the smell of freshly cut grass. A meadow flashed before my eyes. Tinkling laughter teased my senses. My face flickered in my mind. No, not me. Ryker's sister. Love, so much love, coupled with the need to protect, rushed through me. Darkness lit up by a full, proud moon illuminating a new face—my face. A surge of emotion, dark, twisted, hungry, and pure, surged through me, followed closely by love, desire, and, once again, the need to protect.

"I've got you, Serenity," Ryker said into my ear. "Just let go, and let me hold you."

The pain faded, and there was only Ryker—his voice, his arms around me, and his piercing gaze on my face. A breeze ruffled my hair, and the sun ... Oh, God. It was glorious and bright and just as I'd imagined it to be.

"Where are we?"

"You're safe here. This is my safe place," Ryker said.

We were in his mind. We had to be. Somehow, he'd pulled me in.

He hauled me to my feet but didn't release me. "You're hurt, Harker. Real bad. But we're working on it."

"We?"

"Orin, Rivers, and I are healing you."

"And Bane?"

"His power usually knocks you out, and we can't have that right now. We need you to be able to wake up when you're ready. It's the only way we'll know it's working."

Pollen teased my nostrils and blades of grass tickled my feet where I stood. It was real, so real.

"It's going to be all right," Ryker reassured me.

"It was bad. The pain was bad. Do you really think you can heal me?"

His jaw flexed. "I will not let you die." Moisture gathered at the corners of his eyes, but he blinked it away and smiled. "We can just hang out here for a while. Catch up. You've been busy of late with Orin and Rivers and … Bane."

Was that an edge of jealousy in his tone? The images I'd seen when falling into his consciousness flitted through my mind again. I'd seen my face in his mind's eye. The overwhelming emotions of desire and need that had accompanied that image had been all too real, even if this place wasn't. I'd always known he cared about me, but it was because I reminded him of his sister, wasn't it? He'd admitted as much ... hadn't he? But these feelings, this wave of covetousness, was new, and for some reason it sent a thrill through me. What the heck was wrong with me? Ryker was my friend, that was all. But my mouth had a mind of its own, asking the question buried deep in my psyche.

"Does it bother you that I had sex with Bane?"

His bicep flexed. "No." He sighed. "Yes." He shook his head. "I don't know."

My heart was thudding so loud it was a drum inside my head. This was my friend, my confidant, my go-to snuggle guy. He'd been my protector from day one. If he said the words, then it would change everything. Best to drop the subject, to bury it and forget it ever came up. But the adrenaline coursing through me had other ideas.

I had to know. "Ryker, I could die. Tell me."

There was no fear in those words. Not here, not while I was with him, my skin caressed by sunlight.

He looked into my face and dropped the

shutter shielding his emotions, and for the first time since I'd known him, his soul was bared to me—a twisted knot of yearning. And even though none of this was real and we weren't physically here, it was suddenly hard to breathe.

"Ryker ... I don't understand ..."

"Fuck it," he said. "You won't remember this when you wake up anyway."

And then his lips found mine in a tentative caress that brought tears to my eyes. He pulled back slightly, his gaze probing. I couldn't move, afraid that doing or saying anything would spook him. He reached up and ran a thumb over my lips. My breath hitched, and his eyes flared. This time, when his mouth descended on mine, it was in a crushing kiss—the first and the final all rolled into one. My chest was tight, my throat constricted with a cocktail of emotions. How could I not have known? How did this escape me? My hands found his broad shoulders, slid into his silken golden hair, and cupped his jaw, not wanting the moment to end. Perfect, this was perfect.

Lilith's laughter echoed in my mind. I pulled away, chest heaving.

Ryker's mask snapped back into place, his emotions tucked away once more. "There's your answer, Serenity. That's how I feel. But nothing will change. I value your friendship too much to risk losing it."

What was wrong with me? How could I

feel this way for Ryker after I'd just shared something precious with Bane? My vision blurred.

"Don't you fucking dare." Ryker's tone was firm. "There is nothing wrong with you. It's me that has the problem. You have a huge heart, Serenity. You're brave and you stick your neck out for the things you believe in. You're passionate and you're always there with the right words, or one of your awesome fucking hugs. It's impossible for us not to be drawn to you."

"Us?"

He lowered his lids. "It doesn't matter. You need to wake up now."

There was a tug in my solar plexus, a gentle coaxing like a warning. "Wait." I grabbed his shirt. "What do you mean? I need to understand."

But his shirt slipped from my grasp, and my body was suddenly heavy.

"Her hand twitched." Rivers's words were a soft breath on the nape of my neck.

Consciousness melted over me, bringing with it the awareness of my surroundings. The hand clasped in mine, the body pressed to my back, the chest snug against my cheek, and the hair tangled in my fingers. I knew that hair, it was Orin's: thick, coarse, and curling. The hand holding mine was slender and strong—Rivers's. I was cocooned between them, like the filling in a sandwich, and there was power steadily flowing into me from every point of contact.

"Harker? Can you hear me?" Bane's voice was wound tight.

Someone exhaled sharply. "She's okay. She's going to be okay." It was Ryker. The bed shifted and then a door slammed.

I opened my eyes. "I can hear you." I sounded like I'd been three rounds solo with a pack of rippers. I sounded like I'd been stabbed in the fucking gut.

Cassie.

Full awareness slammed into me, and I sprang up, or tried to, because several hands were attempting to hold me down.

"Whoa." Orin pulled me against his chest. "Take it easy."

Rivers rubbed my back. "It's under control."

They both sounded weird enough to stop me from struggling to take a good look at them. Orin's eyes were bloodshot. His cheeks were tear-stained, and Rivers's face was pale and drawn. Both guys were topless. They'd been feeding me while Ryker healed me. Something niggled at the back of my mind, the wisps of a dream that slipped from my mental grasp like quicksilver.

Bane fell back into the lone chair at the foot of the bed and buried his head in his hands.

"We thought we'd lost you," Orin said in a

small voice.

"You saved me. All of you." I looked to Bane. "But you couldn't feed me because your power usually knocks me out. You needed me to be able to wake up."

Bane nodded. "Perfect deduction skills, Harker. That's a no to brain damage." He cracked a shaky smile, but it was all too brief before a storm settled on his face. "This is my fault. I let Cassie back onto the team. I can't believe her jealousy would manifest in this way."

Cassie, who wasn't Cassie. "Where is she?"

"In the basement. Ryker's gone to check on her now."

I leaned in and kissed Orin's shoulder and then pressed a kiss to Rivers's cheek. "Thank you for bringing me back, but I need to see Cassie. Now."

"No way," the guys said in unison.

Bane's eyes narrowed. "What is it, Harker? What aren't you telling us?"

"That thing you have locked in the basement. It isn't Cassie."

8

Cassie raised her head to look at me from her position on the floor of her cell. The darkness was gone, hidden. She looked like Cassie again, but I'd seen it. I'd seen her real face and now I needed the guys to see it too.

Ryker had his back to me, but his shoulders rippled with tension at my approach. He'd healed me, opened himself to me, and allowed me to see how *he* saw me. My stomach tightened as a strange feeling of anticipation flooded me, completely unrelated to confronting Cassie — this was linked to Ryker, but I couldn't for the life of me figure out what it was.

He turned to me. "She can't hurt you again. We won't let her."

Cassie turned to me. "I didn't mean to. I thought you were a sucker. That poor human got killed right in front of me. I was in shock, and then I heard a noise, and I spun and attacked. I didn't know it was you until it was too late."

She was banking on the pain having scrubbed my mind of the actual memory. She was hoping I'd be confused and unsure of what I'd seen. Well, she was in for a disappointment.

My smile was a thin, knowing one. "You're good. I give you that. You sound like her and move like her. You even faked giving a shit about Orin. But you fucked up, because although Cassie may be a little self-centered, she was never intentionally cruel. She would rather die than hurt one of us, and she would fight with her last breath to save a human's life."

Bane blew out an angry breath. "The fuck is going on?"

My fists curled around the bars. "You stepped back and allowed that ripper to kill that human, and then you turned on me. You couldn't allow me to tell. So, that leaves the question. Who the fuck are you?"

Cassie snorted. "I should have gone for the throat."

Ryker slammed his fist against the bars, but she didn't even flinch; instead; her animated expression smoothed out into something alien and eerily composed.

"It no longer matters what you think. It no longer matters what you do."

Ryker sucked in a breath. "Cassie?"

"Cassie isn't here right now," the thing in Cassie's body said. "But she's a fighter, I'll give her that. A noble soul. I almost feel sorry for what I must do."

"Then let her go," Bane said. "Whatever it is you want, we can get it for you."

Cassie cocked her head. "If only it were that easy. What we want cannot be given. It must be taken."

"Why? Why Cassie?"

"She was convenient, and we needed information. But she fought. She kept us away from this base. Prevented us from getting what we needed. But she is weak now. Too weak to do much of anything but watch and die." It shrugged. "It doesn't matter now. You cannot stop us."

Us? There were more? Panic closed a fist around my heart, but I pushed it back. Cassie was still in there, which meant there was still hope. We just needed to get rid of this thing inside her. Whatever *it* was.

"What *are* you?" Ryker asked.

"No one. I am no one. But soon, I will have a body of my own. Soon, I will claim my name."

Dammit, I could really do with some advice from Ambrosius right now. My stomach quivered. Could he hear me? He'd called out to me when Cassie had stabbed me. So where was he now? Think, Harker. There had to be a way to force this thing out of Cassie ... like the way I'd forced Oleander's soul back into his body. That was it! His soul had belonged there, so it had been easy. This thing didn't belong inside Cassie, so extracting it should be easy too, right?

It was a long shot, but fuck it. "Open the cell."

"What? No!" Ryker shot Bane a warning glance.

I turned to Bane. "Please. Just trust me."

Inside the cell, Cassie began to chuckle. "Oh, let her in if she wants. I won't hurt her. There's no reason to any longer. I'm happy to simply wait things out. In a short while, this body will be mine and then no cell will hold me."

I gave Bane a pleading look.

"Open it," Bane said to Ryker.

"This is crazy," Ryker said. But he pulled the keys from his pocket and unlocked the doors.

Cassie, not Cassie, didn't even flinch when I stepped into the cell with her, but Bane and Ryker were two rods of tension.

"What the fuck?" Orin appeared behind Ryker with Rivers at his back.

"Harker," Rivers said evenly. "Get out of there."

I ignored them all and focused my attention on the thing inside Cassie's body. Taking a deep breath, I fell into a crouch beside her.

For the first time since entering the basement, something like doubt flitted across her face.

"What are you doing?" she asked.

The aether was all around me—molecules, atoms, and life. Now, to connect to it all and really see what we were up against.

Cassie's eyes widened. "Stop it."

"Sorry, no can do." I grabbed her face and squeezed. The world went hazy and then the darkness was staring at me from behind Cassie's eyes. Cassie thrashed and kicked and clawed at my arms. The cell was suddenly filled with muscle as Bane and Ryker helped to hold her down.

"I can see it. I can see it." It didn't belong; it had to leave. It needed to be torn out. Just like I had with Oleander, I latched onto the thing inside my friend and exerted pressure with my mind, drawing it up through the layers of Cassie it was hiding beneath. Up, until it was hovering just beneath her skin, an inky black mass that pulsed and writhed, eager to be free of my clutches.

"Shit!" Orin said.

"You can't. You can't do this." Cassie kicked out, desperate to be free of my grip.

But I wasn't letting go. Triumph surged up to choke me as I made the final cut, expelling the entity from Cassie's body and sending it spiraling into the aether. Its scream of rage echoed around us for long seconds after it was gone.

Cassie's eyes rolled back in her head, and her breathing grew shallow.

"She's going into shock." Ryker pulled her into his lap and laid his hands on her diaphragm.

Bane pulled me into his arms, holding me against his chest as Cassie thrashed and frothed at the mouth. Orin let out a strangled sob and my eyes burned in sympathy. What had I done? Had I killed her?

"It would have killed her anyway," Bane said. "At least this way she has a chance."

But it didn't look like I'd done her a favor. She looked like she was in agony—a whole load of agony—and the perspiration on Ryker's brow, the tremble in his hand, told me he was tapping the last of his reserves to help her.

"He's out of juice," Rivers said. "Ryker, you need to stop."

Cassie stilled. Her body relaxed, and her breathing evened out.

Ryker slumped back against the bars and closed his eyes. "She's there. She's still there."

"You did it, Harker." Bane pressed a kiss to my head.

I looked up into his somber face. "Yeah, but what the fuck did I just expel?"

Cassie was tucked up in bed, still unconscious but alive. The room was dark; only a single lamp on her bedside was lit. She looked small and frail and not like the vibrant woman I knew. Her hair, which was usually thick and lustrous, sat flat against her scalp and lay lank and listless on the pillow.

Orin stood at the end of her bed. "You saved her life."

"And you guys saved mine."

He nodded. "How long do you think that thing was inside her?"

"I don't know."

He was wondering how much of her behavior had been due to the entity, and how much had been real. He was wondering if she still loved him. And why the fuck did I suddenly feel hollow at the thought? Orin and Cassie belonged together. It was a sentence that would have tripped off my tongue with ease a few weeks ago but hurt to even think now. We had spent a lot of time together in her absence. Cooking and eating scones. Playing card games and just hanging out on patrol. I'd had him to myself. I'd had them all to myself, and I'd gotten possessive, that was all.

I cleared my throat. "I'm sure you guys will work it out." I headed for the door. Ryker was out cold, and he'd need someone when he awoke, and I needed to get out of here. The last thing I needed was to see Orin ministering to Cassie. Damn, I was a horrible person.

Orin gripped my elbow. "Serenity." His

tone was soft and hesitant.

My heart sank. "Don't. You don't have to say anything." I plastered a smile on my face. "We're friends. We'll always be friends."

My gut twisted. Nothing had happened between us, so why were fists squeezing my lungs like concertina bags? I was one messed-up chick. What the heck was wrong with me? *There is nothing wrong with you.* The words flitted through my mind, and a wave of déjà vu assaulted me.

"Yes, we are friends," Orin said. He tucked in his chin and pressed his lips together as if holding back his words.

"I should go check on Ryker. The guy almost killed himself trying to heal me."

Orin nodded, his huge, stormy eyes dark with regret. Or maybe I was imagining it. It didn't matter, he belonged with Cassie. They deserved a chance. I left Orin to it and went in search of my friend.

Ryker cracked open his eyes as I perched by his hip on the bed. Unlike Cassie's room, this one was bathed in light, as if Ryker needed to absorb the rays into his skin to heal. Heck, who knows. Maybe he did.

I stroked his arm. "How are you feeling?"
He groaned. "Kill me."
My lips twitched. Humor. A good sign.

"Thank you for saving my life."

"You're welcome." He tried to push himself up into a sitting position.

"Don't. Just relax. You need to rest."

"How's Cassie?"

"Still unconscious. Orin is with her. Bane's summoned Tristan, so we'll see."

Ryker scanned my face. "You're worried Orin and Cassie will get back together."

"Why would I be worried?" And how the hell could he know that?

A ghost of a smile played on his lips and he closed his eyes. "Never mind."

My impulse was to push this line of questioning, but self-preservation stepped in and clamped my mouth shut. The dynamic of the group was shifting, and I was at the center of it. Examining it would mean acknowledging what was happening. It would mean accepting that Lilith may have been right about me after all, and that was a road best left untraveled for now.

Ryker's eyes drifted shut. His breath deepened and evened out as he slipped into slumber. A surge of protectiveness filled me. I leaned in on impulse and brushed my lips across his.

"Sleep tight, hon."

His brow furrowed, then smoothed out on a sigh.

A soft knock on the door was followed by

Rivers's voice. "Harker? You in there?"

Ryker didn't stir. Leaving him to his recovery, I slipped out of the room to join Rivers in the hallway.

"What's up?"

"Bane wants us in the kitchen. Oleander has cooked up a post-scourge feast. The humans are here too."

"Is Tristan here yet?"

"No. He was in surgery when Bane called."

It was tradition. We fought and then we feasted, but with me getting stabbed and all, Bane had postponed it until now.

"Shouldn't we wait until Ryker is on his feet?"

Rivers shook his head. "It'll be the better part of a week before Ryker is up for much. It's better for team morale to do the meal now. We also need to discuss what the scourge is up to."

"They lured us onto that industrial estate, just like they lured you, Orin, and Ryker to the alley." In the midst of all the getting stabbed, surviving, and then purging Cassie, it hadn't occurred to me to ask about casualties. "How many did we lose?"

"We lost five officers and several humans."

"Shit."

"We'll hold a memorial service in a few days. There's a bigger picture we're missing. But we'll be getting answers soon enough." His eyes leeched of warmth. "I'll be getting answers."

"How's that?"

His lips curved in a sadistic smile. "We bagged a live one."

My pulse was still racing with Rivers's revelation as we made an appearance in the kitchens. Humans were scattered about, perched on chairs, leaning against counters, and crammed into corners holding plates of food. Oleander had gone all out. We had sandwiches and sausage rolls, quiches, slices of beef and pork, and a bowl of fruit. Tea was on tap, and the coffee pot was bubbling away.

Ava broke off her conversation with Bane as we entered, and her face broke into a relieved smile.

I wound my way over to her.

"The humans don't know about Cassie, or that you were stabbed," Rivers whispered in my ear.

I nodded.

"I see you survived." I pulled Ava into a hug.

She gave me a squeeze. "The rippers we

followed headed straight for the closest residential area. We managed to take enough of them out to scare them off. We lost two officers."

"I'm so sorry."

She pressed her lips together. "We knew what we were getting into when we signed up for this gig. Death is always a possibility. Jamie and Stephen knew that. And Aaron ..." She blew out a breath. "At least he died quick."

Was Aaron the human who'd had his throat ripped out? Bane met my gaze over her head and nodded. Yeah. He'd been the one I'd failed to save. A wave of guilt washed over me. If only I hadn't stopped, if only I'd gone in for the kill regardless of Cassie being there. It was stupid, of course. Why would I have done that knowing my teammate was closer, that she had the advantage? But still, the thoughts weighed on my mind.

Rivers's hand closed over my shoulder reassuringly. "There were too many casualties today," he said to Ava. "And the people we lost will not be forgotten. But if we are to survive, then we must celebrate life. We need to be thankful that we survived and that so many of us are still here tonight."

Ava nodded quickly. "You're right. And we need to train harder. Longer. Whatever it takes." She glanced up at Bane for confirmation.

"Whatever it takes," he echoed. He lifted his chin to address the gathered Protectorate and humans. "Please, eat and relax. We have some business to attend to, but we'll be back shortly."

"More tea, anyone?" Oleander held up the teapot.

"Anything we can help with?" Ava asked.

"No. Thank you," Bane said. "This is personal."

He brushed past her and headed for the stairs, and Rivers and I followed.

Cassie had been held in the basement, and there'd been no sign of the Breed member there. So, that begged the question: "Where is he?"

Bane led the way to the back of the mansion, down a narrow flight of forgotten steps to a reinforced steel door. He pressed his palm to the metal, and it opened with a click. We entered a dry stone corridor dotted with red emergency lights.

"What is this place?"

"Our little secret escape route," Rivers said. "These tunnels lead out off the grounds and into various safe houses in Midnight."

"They also lead to what we call PQ." Bane's voice was a rumble of thunder.

"PQ?"

"Permanent quarantine," Rivers supplied in a terse tone.

We came to an intersection and took a right and then a left. A set of steps leading up appeared to our left, but we strode past those and took the next flight down. We landed in a small lobby cut off by another metal door. Bane pressed his hand to its surface and it clicked open.

"How are you doing that?"

"Palm print recognition," he said. "The door is one huge scanner panel, courtesy of Rivers."

I glanced back at the siren, but his expression was impassive. I'd known he was good at building stuff, but this was some high-tech shit. "I'm impressed."

Bane snorted. "You ain't seen nothing yet." He pushed open the door and ushered me into the chamber beyond.

The phrase *jaw hitting floor* came to mind as I absorbed my surroundings. Composed of steel, chrome, glass, and flashy buttons, the place looked like a secret evil lair, except we weren't evil. The floor was tiled. Monitors and screens lined the far wall. To my left and right were fluid-filled, tubular glass chambers that stretched up to the ceiling. And inside were people … creatures, nephs, whatever. Damn, this was some messed-up shit.

"They're alive in suspended animation." Rivers ran a hand over the runes welded to the glass. "A combination of technology and old magic. There aren't many nephs in Arcadia who know how to charge and use runes any longer."

I looked up at his sharp profile softened only by the curve of his lips and the sweep of his lashes. "So, who made these?"

"I did."

"Seriously? How did I not know this?"

"It isn't something we advertise," Bane said. "Not many people know about this place or about Rivers's affinity with runes. Just the primaries, excluding Cassie, and now you."

They hadn't told Cassie? "Why bring me in?"

Bane arched a brow. "You want out?"

"God, no. I just wondered."

"You've done enough to be brought into the circle of trust."

Wasn't going to argue with that. "Who are these nephs?"

"Dangerous immortals that we've succeeded in taking out of the equation," Bane supplied.

Unkillable nephs. Damn.

A pale blue glow caught my eye. It was emanating from the upper glass half of a door across the room. I wandered over and peered inside. A huge male floated in a massive tank beset with glowing runes. This neph was huge— even larger than Bane. His hair was wound into dreadlocks and floated around his face, which, even though it was distorted by fluid, was cut-glass perfect.

"Who is that?" I tapped the glass.

"Someone ancient," Bane said tersely. "Powerful."

"Hence the extra runes," Rivers said.

"What happens if he wakes up?"

Rivers shrugged. "Then we're fucked."

"But we're not here for him or the others," Bane said. "We're here for The Breed." He strode over to another door and pushed it open to reveal a smaller cell room. The Breed member sat in one of the cages.

His lip curled when he saw us. "Fuck you. Fuck you all. I ain't telling you shit."

The fact they'd brought him here meant that they wouldn't be letting him walk away. They'd probably had to bring him here because the cells in the basement had been occupied by Cassie. It was a shame for him, because if his journey had ended in the basement then maybe he'd have been allowed to live once they'd extracted the information they needed.

From the look on his face, though, he didn't give a shit. No, wait, what was that behind his hostile expression? A flash of fear. A glint of doubt. Yes, this we could work with.

I crouched to get to his eye level. "How are you doing it? How are you controlling the scourge?"

He hawked and spat on the ground. "Fuck you, bitch."

Rivers growled low in his chest. A primal sound that made the hair on the back of my neck quiver in fear and my stomach flip in anticipation.

"And fuck you too." He spat at Rivers.

But there wasn't much conviction in his words.

I smiled. "Tough talk for a guy in a cell. Spout off all you want, but this can only go one of two ways for you—minimal pain or excruciating pain."

He was breathing heavily now. "What does it matter? I'm dead regardless."

"Yeah, you're dead," Rivers said. "But the difference is we could make it quick."

The Breed member sat up straighter. "The Breed does not fear pain. Come in here and try your torture. See how far you get."

Rivers's smile sent a chill of terror down my spine, and it wasn't even directed at me. This was the stoic, calm member of the group who avoided unnecessary confrontation. The one I'd have labeled *least likely to maim for the fuck of it*. Right now, he was a predator, a lithe, wiry predator. His lean face took on a hawkish air, and his eyes were like dark pieces of flint.

The Breed member seemed to deflate somewhat under that smile.

Rivers cocked his head, looking more and more like a bird of prey. "Oh, I don't need to come in there."

That smile again. Damn, I had goose bumps.

"Rivers?" Bane's tone was light, but there was no ignoring the slight edge to it.

Rivers didn't break eye contact with The Breed member. "I'm fine."

"Okay." Bane stepped back and crossed his arms.

It looked like this was Rivers's show to run as he saw fit. Rivers's cropped, silver hair glinted as he walked over to the wall and flipped open a metal panel. He pressed a couple of buttons, and tiny runes flared to life on the cell bars.

The Breed member's eyes widened in shock. "Runes?" He stared at Rivers in awe. "You're a rune speaker?"

Rivers graced him with an unblinking stare. "How are The Breed making the scourge work with them?"

Our prisoner shook his head.

Rivers exhaled, and the runes began to flicker. The Breed member began to gag. He grabbed at his throat, eyes bugging. The runes stopped flickering, and the guy slumped forward, gasping for breath.

"How are The Breed making the scourge work for them?" Rivers asked again.

The guy shook his head, and once more, Rivers used the runes to steal the air from his lungs. But this time he didn't ease up as quickly, and by the time he was done, the guy was on his back, red-eyed and trembling.

"Tell me what I need to know, and I'll end

it quick. I'll stop your heart and be done with it. But defy me, and I'll play with you for days."

His tone was almost conversational, as if he were talking about the weather, but his pale eyes were all pupil. He liked this. He was enjoying being in control.

This wasn't Rivers. This was someone else. This was a cold-blooded torturer. I tried to catch Bane's eye, but he was transfixed with Rivers. I couldn't blame him, because like this, the neph was mesmerizing to watch.

The Breed member pulled himself up. "I don't know how we're doing it." His voice was a croaky whisper. "I just go where I'm told to and kill who I'm ordered to."

"*Tut, tut.*" Rivers shook his head. "Well, that's hardly heart-stopping information, is it?"

The runes began to flicker.

"Please!" The man held up a hand. "I'll tell you all I know. It all started a few months ago. Maximilian decided it was time to form new alliances."

"What kind of alliances?" Rivers pressed.

"The rippers and suckers, for starters. I don't know how he did it, but they started listening to us. He told us they were our eyes and ears above ground. He started taking risks."

"Risks?"

His gaze flicked to me. "Like when he sent us to retrieve the two neph. Several of us felt it was a waste of resources to spend so much time on a personal vendetta. The Breed is about the good of the group as a whole. We'd helped him avenge his lover already. We didn't expect to do it again."

"But you did it anyway."

He nodded. "Yes. He promised big changes, that we would rise above ground, that we would be revered."

"And you believed him."

He swallowed hard. "Not him … but the *thing* inside him."

My pulse lurched, but Rivers didn't skip a beat.

"Explain."

He shook his head. "I can't. We didn't see anything, but we all sensed it. There is another presence."

Like Cassie. Max was like Cassie. "Where is Max? Where is your leader?"

A breeze tickled the back of my neck.

His eyes widened. "Max is no longer our leader."

The hairs on the back of my neck rose in awareness. I glanced over my shoulder, and darkness flitted in the corner of my vision.

"There's something here," Bane said.

"No." The Breed guy held up his hand. "No!"

The runes began to flicker wildly.

"Rivers, what are you doing?" Bane demanded.

A flash of alarm flitted across Rivers's face. "It's not me."

The Breed member in the cell fell to the ground, hand at his throat, clawing and writhing, desperate for just one hit of oxygen. Rivers pounded at the metal panel, trying to override the runes, but the flickering intensified in defiance.

The Breed guy stopped moving, eyes wide and unseeing, and the runes winked out.

A shadow shot through a wall to my left and was gone.

"What the fuck just happened?" Bane asked no one in particular.

It was obvious to me. "It was the same kind of entity that was inside Cassie. It killed him before he could tell us more."

"And Max is infected too," Rivers said.

"But he's no longer in charge of The Breed," Bane added.

I placed my hands on my hips. "Then who the heck is?"

Bane tensed, his head whipping up to stare at the ceiling.

I followed his gaze. "What is it?"

"Nothing." Bane walked to the door. "Rivers, can you finish up here? I need to speak to Harker alone."

Rivers nodded. "Go. I got this." The runes burned red, and the body in the cell was incinerated in a matter of seconds.

He was in his element here. This was his domain, his sanctuary, and the power suited him.

Bane hurried me out of the tunnels and up the steps.

I glanced over my shoulder as we reached the door that would lead back into the mansion. "What's the rush?"

"Abbadon is on the roost. He needs to speak to us, urgently."

"How can you know that?"

"I just do."

"You can communicate with them in your head?"

"No words, just feelings and images."

I grabbed his hand as he went to move past me. "Wait. Is this why you haven't told the others about the Black Wing visits?"

He pushed open the door and ushered me into the stone stairwell leading up to the main floor. "Nephs don't have much time for Black Wings. They don't trust them. And who can blame them. All they do is sit up in their cliff house and watch the carnage. It's best to keep my interactions with them to myself."

"But *you* trust them?"

He snorted. "Trust is a strong word. I use the connections I have to keep the MPD functioning. Abbadon has been useful in the past. He isn't like the others."

Was he referring to the fact that Abbadon patrolled Midnight and helped humans?

Bane gripped my chin and tilted my face up to him. "You know, don't you?"

Urgh. He was in my head again. But just to be on the safe side: "Know what?"

"That Abbadon likes to play savior."

Yep, he knew. "He kinda saved my arse the first time I ventured into Midnight. I was almost captured by The Breed."

He released me. "Well, now I have that to thank him for." He didn't sound happy. We continued up the stairs. "Let's go see what the Black Wing wants."

"What took you so long?" Abbadon's lips were turned down, his wings twitchy. The guy was on edge.

"What do you want, Abbadon?" Bane asked.

"I need your help." He ran a hand over his face. "Correction. The White Wings need your help."

Had I just heard right?

"Is this some kind of joke?" Bane went from irritated to annoyed in the span of a millisecond.

"I wish it was," Abbadon said. "I've just spoken to Gabriel. He has requested MPD assistance on a murder investigation."

Bane went still. "A murder?"

"Yes."

"In Dawn?"

Abbadon nodded slowly.

Dawn was peace. Dawn was safety. The idea of something as heinous as a murder was preposterous. "That's impossible. The humans in Dawn are all silvered, and the White Wings wouldn't compromise their advantage by killing off their flock."

Abbadon turned his attention to me. "Which is why it's such a shock. Three humans have been murdered in the space of two weeks. The White Wings have been unsuccessful in rooting out the killer. They are unfamiliar with the human psyche. Human emotion and motivations are alien to them."

"So, you need *us* to investigate." Bane sounded less than convinced.

Abbadon nodded. "The victims are all members of the same White Wing harem, and due to the high security afforded to a harem, we believe the murderer may be part of that harem. The White Wings have kept the deaths as quiet as possible."

Ah, the harems ... shit, Jesse had been about to join a harem. What if this was Jesse's harem they were talking about? My blood turned to ice. What if Jesse was a victim?

I grabbed Bane's wrist. "We have to do

something."

The sudden urgency in my tone had him frowning. He scanned my face, looking for cues, and then his brow smoothed out.

He turned to Abbadon. "We'll help, but if it's quiet they want, then us barging in as MPD will immediately draw attention."

Abbadon's perfect lips curled in a thin smile. "Not if you go in as ambassadors of Midnight. The official line will be that you're there to discuss opening lines of communication between Dawn and the humans of Midnight. To offer the humans a chance to make a choice for salvation."

As much as I wanted his plan to work, it was ridiculous. The nephs' purpose was to keep the humans out of White Wing clutches and make sure free will wasn't compromised. "Does this Gabriel seriously think the White Wings will buy that?"

Bane and Abbadon exchanged glances.

I threw my hands up. "What?"

"They'll buy it," Bane said. "Their arrogance blinds them. They believe in their cause so completely it will seem perfectly reasonable to them that we're finally backing down."

Okay, so we had a way in. But wait. "If the killer is part of the harem, then how the heck are we, as ambassadors, meant to get in to investigate?"

Abbadon's cerulean gaze was now on me. "That's the second part of the plan. If we are to be successful, we'll need someone in the thick of it. We'll need a wolf among the hens."

"What are you talking about?"

"You, Serenity. We'll need you to go undercover to infiltrate the harem. We'll need you to play at being human again."

Abbadon wanted me to hide my nature, to fake being human, and there was only one way to do that. My daimon bristled, and panic gripped me. Jesse was in Dawn. Jesse could be in trouble, but I'd made a vow to my daimon, a vow to myself, not to use the shield ever again.

The daimon shifted, restless, at the back of my mind.

Don't worry, I reassured her. *I remember my promise.*

Jesse meant the world to me, but we'd have to find another way to solve this case. I raised my chin. "I can't do that. I'm sorry."

Abbadon looked to Bane and then back to me. "I don't think you realize what's at stake here. Murder should not be possible in Dawn. The White Wings exude peace, actually *exude* well-being. The air itself is harmony, and the silvered have had their negative traits muted. Murder is a crime of passion, of madness and insanity, and there are no such things in Dawn. If there is a murderer in Dawn, then the killer is being driven by forces stronger than an angel's power. And that, Harker, is something we do not want to allow to flourish."

His words niggled at my mind. The line about being driven by forces … a force like the entity that had been inside Cassie! I turned to Bane to see the same revelation in his eyes.

"What is it?" Abbadon asked. "What aren't you telling me?"

Bane filled him in on Cassie, The Breed, and Max.

Abbadon pinched the bridge of his nose. "This is bad. Really bad. Is it the one entity, or several?"

"We don't know," Bane said.

But I did. "More than one. The one who'd been inside Cassie implied there were more of them."

"Could these entities be linked to the haunting?" Abbadon pondered out loud.

He was wondering if they were ghosts. "They're not ghosts, they're something else."

"But could it be related?" Abbadon pressed.

Bane shrugged. "We don't have enough information to determine that for certain." Bane tucked in his chin. "Jonathan was murdered by a ripper, and my gut tells me it's all connected somehow. Oleander, our resident ancient, is deciphering Jonathan's notebooks as we speak."

Abbadon blinked in surprise. "Jonathan is dead?"

Bane nodded.

The Black Wing's expression softened. "He was a good soul."

"Yeah, he was."

"What are you looking for in the books?"

"A reference to someone or something called the piper?" Bane said.

I studied the play of emotion on Abbadon's face. The name rang a bell with him. "You know who that is, don't you?"

"Yes. Surely you've heard the story of the pied piper who came into a town and played his flute and had all the children follow him, never to be seen again?"

It rang a bell. "Yeah, but what has that got to do with anything? Jonathan's note said to summon the piper, so you're saying he wants us to summon some guy who plays the flute?"

I didn't think Abbadon's alabaster skin could get any paler. "The piper wasn't a man. The story is a metaphor for death in a time when sickness was rife. The adults in a village of dead children called to death, who swept through the streets, playing his sweet melody to lure the tiny souls into eternal slumber."

"Wait, are you saying the piper *is* death?"

Abbadon nodded slowly.

"Jonathan wanted us to summon death," Bane said, clarifying it out loud. "Death to claim back souls." He glanced up sharply. "To lure the ghosts away from Midnight?"

Abbadon began to pace. "Death has to be our final option. Once he is summoned, he will not leave willingly."

"Jonathan is dead," Bane snapped. "And he used his final moments to leave us a note telling us to summon the piper. We can't just ignore it."

"I never said we should ignore it. Just that it must be a final course of action. I don't believe the hauntings are related to the murders in Dawn. Ghosts, we would have detected, because they are essentially lost souls. I believe that you may be right, that this entity or one of these entities is responsible for the killings, which is why we need to do everything in our power to stop it."

His attention was back on me, probing and insistent.

Every atom in my body wanted to agree to do what they needed. To help catch this fucker. But my promise to my daimon couldn't be disregarded. "I made a vow to my daimon that I would never shut her out again. I can't break that vow."

Abbadon cupped my shoulders and looked deep into my eyes. "The scourge attacks spiked in Midnight, and now we discover that Max was under the influence of an entity all that time? Cassie stood by and allowed a human to be slaughtered, and now we have murders in Dawn. This entity's agenda is linked to death, and if we're going to derail its plan, then we need to stop these killings."

Bane locked gazes with me over the Black Wing's shoulder. "You managed to expel the entity from Cassie's body. You might be the only one who can stop this thing. The only one who can see it."

Fucking hell. Talk about pressure.

The tightness in the back of my mind eased, and my diamon's assent spread through me like melted butter. *Just this once*, it said. *To protect the innocent. Just this once.*

I sagged in Abbadon's grip. "I have permission to do it."

He released me with a sigh of relief. "Good. You leave tomorrow. They've prepared for three MPD and a human tribute."

I guess I was the tribute.

Showered and wrapped in my robe, I searched my wardrobe for something that screamed human tribute. Leather, Lycra, and denim glared back at me defiantly. Bane had instructed me to look demure and unthreatening. I needed a simple dress, something cream or white. But dresses weren't my thing. Did I even own one? Maybe Cassie would have something I could borrow? Orin had popped in earlier to tell me she was conscious and alert. Tristan had been to see her in the early hours of the morning while I'd been asleep.

A short rap on the door interrupted my musings. "Come in."

I grabbed a pair of jeans and a tank top, then shut the wardrobe. I turned to find Rivers standing in the doorway.

"Hey."

He stepped into the room and shut the door behind him. "Bane thought you may need a top-up before you bring the shields down." A ghost of a smile played on his lips. "A little treat for your daimon for being so accommodating."

My daimon purred in appreciation. "Just give me a moment to get dressed and—"

"No need." He walked toward me and my insides clenched in awareness.

This wasn't the reserved Rivers I was used to. This was the persona he'd donned in the secret lair—the hawk man with the unflinching, penetrating gaze and the icy confidence to do what needed to be done. I took a step back on reflex and then locked my knees to prevent another. What was I doing? This was Rivers. There was nothing to be afraid of. And yet my stomach quivered in warning as he came to stand inches in front of me. The air between us fizzed and popped. His attention was on my mouth, my neck, my chest, and then on the lip of the robe covering my breasts. His throat bobbed, the only sign of the Rivers I knew.

"I need to touch you," he said.

I let out a choked laugh. "You'll find it's me that needs to touch you to feed."

He dragged his gaze from my chest back up to my face, and our gazes locked tight. "No. I *need* to touch you."

"Oh." The word was a tiny explosion of breath.

"Slide the robe off," he said. "Slide it off so I can see you."

It wasn't a request. It was a command. I didn't do commands, except I was complying. I was shrugging the robe off my shoulders. It slid down, barely covering my breasts, leaving me exposed to his hungry, predatory gaze. He cupped my bare shoulders and slowly slid his hands down my arms and then back up again. It was a simple caress but sexy as hell.

"Rivers, I—"

"Quiet." It was a breathless demand.

I snapped my mouth closed. The pulse at my throat pounded as his fingers skimmed my collarbones. The heels of his hands brushed the tops of my breasts, and heat spiked through me, igniting a slow throb between my legs.

He leaned in. "Open the robe, Serenity. I need to see all of you."

What was I doing? Why was I doing this? Because I wanted him to see me. To see the heat rise in his cheeks and watch his eyes darken. I slowly undid the tie and let my robe fall open. His breath caught, and his scent, an electric storm, spiked. He closed his eyes and pressed his forehead to mine.

"Fuck, you're beautiful."

I needed him to touch me, to run his fingers over my skin, teasing the electricity between us. He pulled back, and tilted my chin with the crook of his finger. His pupils were huge, reflecting only me. He leaned in and ran his tongue along the crease of my mouth. I opened for him and he claimed me. His hand cupped the back of my neck, holding me immobile while he assaulted my mouth with his tongue and teeth, sucking and nipping and making love to it. My nerves were on fire. Heat raced through my veins as I struggled to get the upper hand. My back slammed into the wardrobe door, and the full length of his body pressed up against me. Fabric rubbed against my freshly scrubbed skin, the friction heightening the pleasure. Fingers dug into my flesh, my shoulders, my arms, and my waist, and then up to cup my breasts. Oh, fuck. What was he doing to my nipples with his clever fingers? Every tug, every roll, drew at my core, winding me tighter and tighter. A small part of my brain whispered that this wasn't feeding. This was pleasure, just unadulterated pleasure. But there was no room in my overstimulated brain for those thoughts. The last few weeks, every feeding had been leading up to this, just as it had been with Bane. Lilith, the fucking bitch, had been right.

He broke the kiss and stared down at me with heavy-lidded eyes. "Feed, Harker. Fucking feed." And then he dipped his head to my chest and took my nipple in his mouth. The world shattered, and my daimon latched on and began to feed. Rivers moaned, and his grip on my hips tightened, and then I was being flung onto the bed, and that clever mouth found a new target between my thighs. I reached out to stop him, to push him away. This was too much. All this was too much. It wasn't right, but my daimon was in her element, writhing and bucking and moaning. My hands wound in his hair, and instead of pushing him away I held him to me as he tipped me over the edge with his tongue, while his name tripped off mine, over and over again.

It was over too soon and not soon enough. My cheeks were hot with shame and the after-effects of the orgasm he'd just laid on me. He retreated and straightened his clothes, smoothing a hand over his hair, his face emotionless again, as if nothing had happened. How the fuck did he do that?

I was suddenly aware of how naked I was, laid out like a buffet on the fucking bed. I scrambled up and tightened my robe.

Fuck. I couldn't look at him. "I'm ... I'm sorry. I should have stopped you."

"Did you want to?" Rivers asked.

I swallowed hard. "No." My cheeks heated in shame. "I'm so sorry."

He tipped my chin up to his and stared down at me with those ice chip eyes. "Don't be sorry, Harker. Just stop pretending. You're not human. We're not human, and we're not bound by the same societal conventions. If you stop pretending, then so can we."

We? What did he mean?

He kissed my forehead to soften the

reprimand. "We leave in an hour and a half. Meet you in the foyer."

He strode from the room without a backward glance.

Stop pretending ... I'd spent my whole life being human; how the heck did I shrug it all off?

"The white dress. That's the one," Cassie said.

I located the dress and peeled it off the hanger.

"There are ballet flats in there too, and an Alice band on the dresser if you need it."

"I'm good, thanks."

She made a sound of exasperation. "God. Listen to me, trying to make up for everything by loaning you my stuff. If only *I'm sorry I tried to kill you* could cut it," Cassie said.

I hung the dress over my arm and turned to look at her.

She was propped up against the pillows. The dark smudges under her eyes and her sallow complexion were at odds with the glowing picture of health we'd been witness to the past few weeks. But who knew how this entity worked. It had obviously masked her true appearance somehow. Or maybe, by tearing it free, I'd damaged Cassie.

"Don't look at me like that," she said. "I know I look horrific, but I'll be fine. I can already feel my strength returning." She winced. "Along with every single memory of what I did when it had me."

"None of it was your fault."

She met my gaze levelly. "Yeah, it was. I allowed this to happen. I allowed it to seduce me."

"I don't understand."

She closed her eyes briefly. "At first it was just a voice in the back of my head urging me to do and say things. Telling me it was all right to have Killion as well as Orin, and that Orin's feelings didn't matter as much as mine. I allowed it in when I followed its advice, and once it had me, it was like being in the passenger seat in my own body. It was speaking using my words, making decisions for me, and I knew what it wanted. It wanted to be here. It wanted to be in the know."

"So you left? How did you make it leave?"

"I fought back. I took the driver's seat long enough to say and do things to get it away from here, from you guys."

"Why not use that time to tell us what was happening?"

Her eyes welled up. "I tried so many times, but the words wouldn't come. It was as if they no longer existed. I had no choice but to stay away." She sighed. "I fought as hard as I could but I lost. After Bane fired me, the thing took over, and then I was merely a watcher while it brought me back here and pretended to be me."

I knew better than anyone how powerful a voice in your head could be. How its needs could become entwined with your own. With Ambrosius silent, there was a part of me that felt hollow and lost.

My heart went out to her. All the times I'd thought awful things about her felt like a betrayal now. "You can't blame yourself, Cassie. You couldn't have known that voice wasn't your own."

She leaned back into her pillows. "I guess you're right, because all those thoughts were already there. They were mine. This thing just played on my darkest desires. I wanted Killion and I wanted Orin, but I wanted Killion more and the entity sensed that." She exhaled slowly, as if letting go of the bad memories. "But I'm back now and I'm going to make it up to Orin. I'll forget about Killion. He's never been good for me. Orin is kind and gentle while Killion is a fucking bastard. I'm better off with Orin."

She watched me from under hooded lids as she gave her speech, and my stomach tightened. So, they were definitely getting back together then. I expected as much, but still … to hear her confirm it. She hadn't been herself. Orin couldn't penalize her for that. He was loyal and good, and, of course, he would give her another chance, and … he loved her. Damn. I knew how much he loved her.

"I'm happy for you guys." I finished on a

smile, but the lie sat sluggish and unsavory on my tongue.

The tension around her mouth and eyes eased. "I'm tired." She closed her eyes. "If you see Orin, can you ask him to come see me before you guys leave?"

"Sure. Thanks for loaning me the dress."

My mind was reeling as I stepped out of her room and smacked bang into the man in question himself. Orin's hands shot out to steady me.

"You all right?"

His sea-gray eyes were intense as they probed, trying to read me. Cassie was back, and I may never get to hold him again. Fuck it. I wrapped my arms around his torso and pressed my cheek to his chest. His heartbeat skipped and sped up. This felt good. Right. It felt like home.

"Serenity?" He stroked my hair, his touch tentative, gaining in confidence when I ran a hand up his spine.

"I'm fine. Really good." I pulled back to look up into his face. "I'm glad you're coming with us."

He searched my face, barely breathing. "Serenity, I—"

God, I couldn't hear it from him too. "Cassie told me the good news. I'm happy for you guys."

I pushed up on tiptoes and brushed his cheek with mine. "See you in the foyer in half an hour."

His gaze clouded and then he nodded. "I'm still here for you, Serenity. Whatever you need."

My heart felt like it was melting and breaking at the same time. "I ... I have to go."

I left him to his final check on Cassie and made my way back to my room to change for our trip. My heart ached. It ached for Orin and yearned for Bane and Rivers and coveted Ryker's attention. My heart was a traitorous, confused bitch, because she wasn't content with loving one. She loved them all.

What was I going to do?

The car sidled up the road leading to the pearly gates. They shimmered in the sunset, pink bone fingers reaching for the sky. Bane, Rivers, and Orin all wore sunglasses to protect their eyes. Years of being confined to Midnight had made them sensitive to natural sunlight. It would take time for their eyes to adjust. Mine had adjusted just fine and were drinking in the orange landscape. Damn, I'd missed this — the warmth and the colors.

I was dressed not in my usual Protectorate gear, but in the simple knee-length white dress Cassie had loaned me. Demure but alluring in that it hugged and skimmed my body in all the right places. The heat in Bane's eyes and the appreciation on Orin's face when I'd walked down the stairs into the foyer to meet them had stolen my breath. Even Rivers had done a double take that had made my pulse skip. A surge of protectiveness rose up inside me. I'd do anything to keep these nephs safe, and they'd do the same for me.

Right now, as we drew closer to our destination, backup sounded real good, because I was about to be handed over to the White Wings like chattel. My chest fluttered with nerves. Focus, go over what you know. Okay, only the heavenly bodies, The Powers that governed Dawn, knew of the murders. Apparently, they'd entrusted the investigation to two archangels: Raguel and Michael. Michael was the leader of the archangels. Bane had tried to explain the hierarchy of the divine beings, and the spheres they'd lived on, but honestly, all that mattered was how things operated in Dawn.

In Dawn, The Powers ruled supreme. Before they'd settled in on the earthly plane, their job had been to organize and monitor the movements of the other angels. Warriors by nature, they'd given up their armor and settled in for the long haul, focusing on politics instead of war, which was fine for now. But if war came, Bane assured me they would be a formidable force to be reckoned with. The Powers issued the orders, but the principals were the ones that put them into effect, charging the archangels and angels with the relevant duties. Once protectors, guardians, and educators of the earthly realms, they were now mere middlemen.

The smaller gates set within the larger gates came into view. Built into a gilded arch, they were at least four times the height of Bane, and six meters wide, so not that small really. Silver-liveried White Wings manned the entrance. This was the check point leading into the coveted district of Dawn, and the glimpse of the world beyond was bright blue skies and sunrise. Of course, Dawn was special. It saw the sun rise and set. It felt the kiss of the moon and the shiver of twilight. This wasn't my first visit, but it was the first time I'd be seeing Dawn in daylight.

Bane brought the car to a halt at the gates and waited. Rivers and Orin shifted nervously in the back seat. According to Bane this was Orin's first visit. Rivers, on the other hand, had done some work for the White Wings in the past. I'd questioned what that work had been but Bane had been tight-lipped and changed the subject.

A White Wing strode over to the driver's side, and Bane wound down the window.

"Ambassadors of Midnight bringing tribute," Bane said.

The White Wing ducked his head and scanned the interior of the vehicle, counting heads no doubt. His gaze lingered on me a moment. My pulse kicked, but I forced myself to breathe even and natural. Shields were up, and as far as he was concerned, I was human. It was weird. After being one with my daimon, even though I knew she was just beyond the barrier I'd erected, it was achingly empty without her.

The guard nodded curtly and stepped back. "We've been expecting you." He raised a hand to his comrade at the tower attached to the gate and the air shimmered.

"Wards are down," Orin said from the back seat.

"What now?" Rivers wondered.

"Please exit the vehicle," the guard said.

"We need wheels in there," Bane said.

The guard remained impassive. "Please exit the vehicle, ambassador."

"Bane?" Rivers's tone was saturated with warning.

"It's all right," Bane said.

He unlocked the door and stepped out of the car.

"All of you," the guard clarified.

I reached for my door, but Rivers stopped me with a hand on my shoulder. "Wait."

"What is the meaning of this?" Bane enquired. His tone, to an unpracticed ear, was calm and polite, but to us, used to every timbre of his voice, it was laced with the potential of violence.

The sound of an engine drifted toward us and then a silver van appeared in the gateway.

The doors opened and a White Wing dressed in jeans and a cream T-shirt stepped out. He raised his chin in greeting, and Bane's shoulders relaxed a fraction.

"Looks like that's our ride," Rivers said.

I twisted in my seat. "Who is that?"

"Michael."

"The archangel?"

"The one and only."

He was jogging toward us now, his long, blond hair blowing back from his bearded face.

Bane walked forward to meet him. They clasped hands. Michael's gaze drifted over to our car.

"Please exit," the guard said again.

Rivers and Orin got out at the same time, and then Rivers held my door open for me. He took my hand, his palm cool and dry against mine. We were shielded from view by the bonnet of the car, and this was probably the last time any of them would be able to show affection toward me until this was all over. I was a tribute, a human they'd brought as an offering to the White Wings, a symbol of the sincerity of their proposal. I squeezed his hand and then let go.

He strode ahead of me, jerking his head to indicate I follow his athletic form. Orin was already beside Bane. The two huge, black-clad figures with weapons strapped to their person contrasted starkly with the golden, glowing White Wing. The three men watched as Rivers and I approached. Michael's gaze was the most probing. I was a new plaything for some White Wing, and he was curious to see what the nephs had brought.

"Welcome to Dawn." Michael's voice was smooth like velvet. "You've chosen your tribute well, Bane."

A gentle breeze brushed tendrils of my auburn hair against my cheeks. It was rarely left loose—combat and long hair didn't mix well unless tied back out of the way—and it made me feel soft and vulnerable and exposed. The dress and ballet flats didn't help much either. The whole ensemble screamed weak human, but it was just an outfit—a facade I'd slipped on to allow me to do my job as Protectorate. This wasn't me, but then Michael knew that because he was one of the White Wings in on the secret.

I smiled warmly, maybe too warmly, because Rivers nudged the small of my back in a tone-it-down gesture. I reined it in and lowered my lashes, so I missed it when Michael laughed—the sound was like sunshine and rainbows.

Urgh, where the heck had that comparison come from?

"Come, I'll get you settled in the ambassadors' quarters and then we'll deliver our tribute to her new home."

No mention of the real reason we were here. Too many ears tuned in on our conversation for candor. We piled into the van, Orin and Rivers pressed on either side of me in the back seat and Bane beside Michael in the front. Michael started the engine. The inside of the van was high-tech and sleek, a complete contrast to the town where they held their humans. Sorry, *housed* their humans. But then Bane had explained on our last visit how they kept humans and technology separate, believing it to be a corrupting force.

"Phase one complete," Michael said. "I didn't believe it when Abbadon told me you had a neph who could pass for human." He caught my attention in the rear view mirror. "Your shields are indeed powerful. If I didn't know better, I'd have been fooled."

"Thanks."

Orin's hand slid onto my thigh, palm facing up in invitation. I slid mine into it. His fingers closed around me, solid and reassuring. Rivers surprised me by taking my other hand and running his thumb back and forth across my skin. Gentle now, but earlier, in the privacy of my room, it had been a different story. He'd been in charge, taking what he needed and giving me what I craved.

I caught a glimpse of my face in the rear view mirror, lips parted, cheeks flushed. Exhale and focus, Harker. Damit. This dynamic would need to be examined at a later date.

The van began its descent into the district spread out below—a metropolis of glass towers and stone arches. The roads were pretty silent—probably because White Wings preferred to fly. The van was for our convenience, because, as a rule, neph didn't have wings. Did Michael know that Bane was an exception?

The ground levelled out into a road bordered by tall, lush foliage and trees. The branches swayed and bobbed in the sweet breeze and blossoms floated to the ground like snowdrops.

It was truly beautiful here.

"Whose harem are we investigating?" Orin asked.

Good question. "Yeah, whose harem am I going to be infiltrating?"

Michael turned off the main road and onto a slip road. He met my gaze in the mirror once more. "Mine. You'll be joining my harem."

Valet parking, a tower made of glass and silver, and a trip in an elevator that sported a view of the whole district followed. You could even see the Victorian-modelled towns the White Wings had set up. They looked like tiny play scenes from this height.

We exited onto a lushly carpeted floor and directly into a penthouse suite. Leather seats, a bar, mini library, and rugs that made me want to kick off my boots to feel the thick pile between my toes greeted us. The White Wings had it good.

"This is your suite," Michael said. "There are three bedrooms, all with their own bathrooms. Room service is twenty-four hours. The humans in the kitchens have been trained to cook just about anything your heart desires. You have three days to come up with answers. The staff and the other angels have been told you'll be meeting with The Powers on the third day, and you will, but it won't be to discuss Midnight, it will be to provide us with your findings."

"Sounds reasonable," Bane said. "We'll need a vehicle and free pass to move around the district as we please."

"You have it." Michael pointed at the bar. "There are sigil pins behind the bar. If you wear them, you won't be questioned or stopped." His gaze slid my way. "And now to the most important player of all."

I exhaled, suddenly ridden with nerves.

"Miss Harker, you will be in the midst of the action. You'll need to gain the trust of my harem. You will need to become one of them and find out whatever you can about the murders. I sense there is much they are not telling me."

"How many humans do you have?"

"Ten, you will be the eleventh. There were thirteen …"

Of course, three had been killed.

"Do you have any idea why the victims may have been killed?"

He shook his head.

"You knew them, were intimate with them. Maybe there's something you know that you don't even realize could be important."

He snorted. "I didn't *know* them, Miss Harker. I had sex with them on a regular basis, and that is all."

Wow. What a dick. It was bad enough that

the White Wings saw it fit to have harems, let alone treat the humans in them with such indifference. "I don't understand why you have to do this?"

"Do what? Investigate the killings?" Michael frowned. "I would have thought that was obvious."

I rolled my eyes. "No. Keep harems. You're fucking White Wings. God charged you with watching over humans. He didn't charge you with fucking them."

Michael's amiable expression slipped and his face darkened. "Well, God isn't here anymore, and living on the mortal plane has its consequences."

"What the heck is that supposed to mean?"

"Harker, enough," Bane warned.

"No. I want him to explain." I crossed my arms. "Go on, justify yourself. How did you go from protector to abuser?"

"Abuser? Is that what you think we do?"

I blinked in surprise at the anger in his tone.

"Michael, she doesn't understand," Bane reasoned.

Michael exhaled through his nose. "Yes. I can see that." His focus was back on me, intense and forbidding. "Living on the mortal plane comes with consequences: urges, needs, desires, and cravings. And for a White Wing, if not satisfied, these consequences can lead to fury and destruction."

"And the humans? Do they get a choice?" Jesse's face came to mind. She'd seemed happy about joining her lover's harem, but what if it hadn't turned out how she expected? "Or do you court them and pretend to care to trap them into signing up?"

Michael shrugged. "We do what we must, but a human is free to leave if unhappy." His lips curled in a superior smile. "But none of *my* harem have ever chosen to leave."

I returned the smug smile. "No. They just get murdered instead."

Orin cleared his throat to mask a laugh. But Bane shot me an annoyed glance. Okay, maybe I needed to stop being so judgmental. If the humans were happy, then …

"You'll see for yourself soon enough," Michael said. "After the bedding ceremony, I'll introduce you to my women."

"Bedding ceremony?" Bane's tone was tight. "No one is bedding anyone."

Rivers was instantly on alert, and Orin took a step closer to me, putting me in his shadow.

Michael waved a dismissive hand. "It's nothing to be concerned about. I don't intend to actually bed your officer, Bane. Everyone merely needs to believe I have."

Bane didn't look reassured; if anything, his muscles tensed even more, biceps jumping as if desperate to take a swing. But it was Rivers who responded.

"You touch her without her consent, and I will personally rip off your wings." Rivers ended on a chilling smile. The predatory gleam I'd witnessed in the underground lair was back.

Michael held up his hand in a conciliatory gesture. "Put the daggers away, Mind Reaper. My intentions are honorable."

Rivers blanched and dropped his gaze.

"Mind Reaper?" I looked from Rivers to Michael.

"We should get started," Bane said. "When is this bedding ceremony?"

And suddenly everything was cool? Huh? What the heck?

"This evening," Michael said. "In the meantime, I'll leave the *tribute* with you. Feel free to explore the district. I'll be back to collect Miss Harker when the sun sets, and Raguel will take you to examine the victims' bodies." He smiled wryly. "I'm afraid that until Miss Harker extracts some useful leads from the ladies in my harem, you nephs are no real use in the investigation. Until then, you will play your part and act as if you are learning about Dawn in order to convey its wonders to the humans of Midnight."

"Yeah, we get it," Orin said.

So, it was up to me. If I couldn't get friendly with these humans, then we were fucked. The lift slid shut behind Michael, and I was alone with the guys.

I turned on Rivers. "Mind Reaper? Why did he call you that?"

Rivers walked into the nearest bedroom and shut the door.

Bane pinched the bridge of his nose. "Knowledge is power, but sometimes you need to just take the cues and not ask the questions."

"Bane, it's not her fault," Orin said.

Bane sighed. "No. It's Michael stirring shit as usual."

Was anyone going to actually explain to me what was happening here? Bane's stern face screamed no, but Orin. Orin could never say no to me. I turned to him now, and he looked to Bane. What for? For permission?

"You know what. Forget it." I strode over to Rivers's room, knocked on the door, and entered. If I'd done something to upset him, asked a question I shouldn't have, then I needed to make it right.

Rivers stood with his back to me, his attention on the panoramic view of the district.

"I'm sorry if I upset you." I hovered by the door. "Just forget I asked, okay?"

His shoulders sagged. "No. You were going to find out at some point anyway. I want you to know. I just needed a minute." He turned his head, offering me his profile. "Mind Reaper is a nickname from my time before."

"Before what?"

"Before here." His shoulders rose and fell. "Sometimes we'd catch White Wings, and when we did, it was my job to extract information from them." His tone was flat, emotionless. "When we came here, to Arcadia, I used the same skills on the supremacy, a group of fanatical nephs who wanted to rule Midnight."

He'd been a torturer?

"I was good at what I did," he continued. "I never got my hands dirty, not once, because I could make them do everything to themselves."

Oh, God. He'd used his siren voice on them. Made them hurt themselves. Cut themselves.

"I enjoyed the power." He turned to face me. "Does that scare you? Disgust you?"

Did it? He looked torn, part hopeful and part anxious. As if he wanted me to shun him, to validate what he was thinking about himself, yet needed me to absolve him. All I saw was the man I'd come to care deeply about. I finally understood that tightly controlled demeanor and the flash of the predator beneath his pretty skin. How could I shun him for taking on a role that needed to be filled in a time of desperation and chaos?

"No, Rivers." I took a step toward him. "You don't scare or disgust me. You did what you had to."

His eyes glinted silver. "Yes, I did. But I didn't have to enjoy it so damn much." The words were a raw admission, and he closed his eyes briefly, breathing evenly through his nose to center himself.

Shit, this was really cutting him up. "Do you miss it?"

He blinked in surprise. "What?"

"Do you miss being the Mind Reaper?"

His irises flicked to the left as he considered my question. "No. No, I don't. But I think he misses being in control." He swallowed hard. "I can feel him beneath my skin, itching to get out. I worry what will happen if he ever gets out again."

Yes. I'd seen a glimpse of this Mind Reaper in the lair. The eager way in which he'd extracted information from the Breed guy. But he couldn't live like this, in fear, all the time. Wound tight and always in control.

I bridged the gap between us. "You did what you had to in a dark time. You did what needed to be done for the Black Wings and the nephs to survive." I reached up to cup his cheek. "And you're no longer the Mind Reaper. But he is a part of you, an essential part. Don't fight him; let him integrate with you, let him become Rivers. My Rivers."

He closed his eyes and leaned into my caress. "Say it again."

My chest grew tight and my pulse fluttered. "You're my Rivers."

His lips found mine and he breathed me in.

The kiss lasted mere seconds but it was packed with every emotion that the siren was feeling. Guilt, relief, desire—I absorbed it all.

He broke away and cupped my face. "I'm not him anymore, but I meant what I said to Michael. If he touches you without your consent, I *will* hurt him." He closed his eyes and pressed his forehead to mine. "I'll become the Mind Reaper to protect you."

My attention dropped to the silver cuff on his wrist, his power muter.

He followed my gaze and a wry smile twisted his lips. "You know about that, huh?"

"Yes. You made a vow."

"I did, and I never thought anything would convince me to break it." He stroked my cheek with his thumb. "And then I met you. You reminded me of her, of my failure, of the horror I've committed. But you're not her. You're entirely you. Impossible, improbable you."

A lump formed in my throat under his intense regard.

A knock on the door interrupted the moment. "Harker, Rivers. We're moving out," Orin said.

Rivers reluctantly released me. "Let's go see how the Winged fuckers live."

We sat sipping creamy coffee in a little cafe on the corner of an immaculate street. We'd spent an hour and a half exploring the area around the tower we were housed in. Neatly clipped grass, trimmed trees, and clean chrome and glass buildings were the signature of the main district. This was where the angels lived. The only humans who lived here were the ones employed to run the small businesses—the eateries and cafes. On the heavenly plane they hadn't needed to eat or drink, but here in the mortal realm, it seemed the divine beings had developed a taste for good food, wine, and coffee. They *really* liked their coffee. The air practically reeked of freshly ground beans. It was heady and intoxicating, and it was what had drawn us to this tiny coffee house.

The sun lanced in through the windows, glinting off shiny chrome surfaces and highlighting Bane's face. He sat opposite me, his shades off and tucked into the collar of his T-shirt. I'd seen him in lamplight, bathed in sunset, and kissed by the moon, but in the midday light he was gloriously larger than life. Every plane and angle of his face was sharper, and his violet irises stood out starkly against his tanned skin.

"Quit staring, Harker." His voice was a delicious vibration against my senses.

Orin chuckled. "Aw, look. He's blushing."

"Fuck you, Orin," Bane said with a smile.

I ducked my head. Getting distracted by the guys was not an option right now. This thing we had between us would have to wait to be explored. Right now, three humans were dead. That was why we were here. To find the killer, to expel the entity, and to maybe get some answers as to what we were dealing with.

"We're not here to sightsee. This is a waste of time." I pushed my coffee away. "We need to get back to the quarters and demand to see the bodies right now. This is our investigation, and if they keep dictating when we can do shit then we're going to fail. Look, this entity could be in any of them."

Bane sat forward. "Fucking hell. You're right."

"Michael's harem is being killed off," Orin said.

I nodded slowly. "And who has unlimited access to them but him."

Rivers shook his head. "It's not him. If it was, he would have covered it up better."

True. "But it could be one of the other angels in the know, like this Raguel, or the angel running the autopsies, or one of The Powers. So far, we're assuming the killer is human. But if the entity can claim a neph, then what's to say it can't claim a White Wing." I sat back and slammed my hand on the table. "This is our investigation and we need to take charge."

Bane drained his cup. "Let's go find the morgue."

The morgue was a tiny building on the border closest to the Victorian town where the majority of humans lived. Angels had no need for ministrations of death, but humans did. The human mortician, aptly named Morty, as if his parents had suspected what his profession would be, was a stickler for protocol.

He crossed his arms and stood his ground, glaring at Bane from beneath bushy brows. "The appointment is for six p.m., and you are to be accompanied by Raguel," he said for the third time.

From the tick of Bane's jaw, to the flare of Rivers's nostrils, I could tell the guys were about to lose it with this tiny, stubborn man. Even my blood was heating in annoyance. Orin, however, was as cool and calm as ever. He caught my eye and canted his head toward Morty. What did he want me to do? He widened his eyes as if to nudge me into action. I guess a feminine touch couldn't hurt.

It was time for a little cajoling. "Look, you know that we're here to help, right?"

He blinked at me, taking in my clothes, my hair, and my tentative smile.

"Since when does the MPD recruit humans?" he said stiffly.

"Since the humans stood up and demanded to be permitted to protect themselves. These are our people dying, not theirs. Do you think they really care about a few mortal lives?"

He blinked slowly. "They summoned you, didn't they?"

"Yes, they did. But I doubt it's because the dead have value. I wager it's more to do with the fact that death is bad for business. If it gets out that there is a murderer in Dawn, then how many humans would want to become silvered? How many silvered would fight to leave?" His mouth parted as if to respond, but I rushed on. "We care about these women. We want to find the murderer, not just to stop a PR nightmare, but to save lives."

He swallowed. "But Raguel said—"

"Why wait when we can get started? What expertise can Raguel bring to the table that you and we don't already have?" I cocked my head. "If he cared so much he wouldn't be off selecting new women for his harem. He'd have brought us straight to you, because this ... this is important."

The mortician balked. "He's recruiting for his harem?"

Aha, knew that would get under his skin. "That's what we were told." Liar, liar, pants on fire.

He pulled himself up to his full height. "Well then, I guess we *should* get started."

He led us deep into the building, through several doors, and into a chilly corridor and then a room lined with silver drawers. The bodies were laid out on gurneys side by side. They were ice cold to the touch, and the pale blue skin and dark blue lips reminded me of the kelpies in their unglamoured form. These had been living, breathing humans once, and now they were slabs of meat on a metal tray.

"Cause of death, for Gemma is blunt weapon trauma to the back of the head," Morty said, indicating the first victim. "Sarah here has a stab wound to her carotid artery, and Caroline was asphyxiated."

So, no pattern in the manner they were killed. I studied the bodies for a long moment, the fingers, the hands, and the nails.

"No defensive wounds? Which means there was no struggle."

Morty held up a finger. "Good catch. Yes. With the blunt force trauma, it makes sense; she may not have seen the killer coming. But from the angle of the carotid stab wound, the killer would have been directly in front of the victim."

"She would have seen her killer?"

"Unless she was sleeping," Rivers said.

"Time of death for Sarah is between nine p.m. and three a.m. She could have been awake or asleep."

"And Caroline? Do we have any idea how the killer may have suffocated her?"

Morty pointed out the slightly darker blue marks on her face. "A hand held over her nose and mouth."

"Then where are the defensive wounds? Is there any skin under the fingernails?"

Morty shrugged. "There is none, but ..." He pointed at the ligature marks on her wrists. "She may not have had use of her hands."

Wait. She'd been tied up? "The killer had tied her up and then suffocated her."

Morty nodded.

"But no defensive wounds or skin under her nails means she didn't fight the killer when he or she tied her up. Which means she probably knew her killer, maybe even allowed herself to be tied up." Like in a kinky sex game? "Morty, do you know who has access to the harems?"

Morty frowned. "I'm not sure. It varies from harem to harem. You would need to ask Michael."

"What are you thinking, Harker?" Bane asked.

"I'm wondering if the ladies in the harem were sleeping with anyone else."

Morty snorted. "And risk their harem master's wrath?" He shook his head. "It would be a foolish move."

"One that might get them killed?" Rivers proposed.

Morty's brows shot up. "Oh. I suppose there could be relations between the men and women in the harem, but it is prohibited."

Wait. What? Michael had men in his harem?

"White Wing sexuality is fluid," Bane said.

Damn my shitty poker face.

But then my mind was whirring. The entity that had taken over Cassie had played on her hidden desires, her wants and needs, and amplified them. It had made her take actions she wouldn't have otherwise, and once she'd set foot on that path, it had claimed her. If an entity had somehow infiltrated Dawn and managed to latch on to someone in the harem, it would aim for someone with hidden demons. Someone with hidden desires it could manipulate. This person had used three very different methods to kill these women, but it was Caroline who gave us the most clues. She'd allowed herself to be tied up, I was sure of it. And my gut told me that it had been in sex-play.

"We need to find out about Caroline." I looked up at Bane. "We need to find out if she was into women as well as men, because if she wasn't, then we know our killer is male, and we can narrow down our list of suspects to the men in Michael's harem."

"And if she was into women too?" Rivers asked.

"Then we find out which woman she was into."

"It's going to be up to you now," Orin said. "You've got three days to gather as much information as you can. We're here when it's time to take that thing down."

I nodded, my stomach suddenly queasy. I'd felt the pressure of harmony in the air. The sweet ripples of peace that floated on the breeze. My Black Wing blood afforded me some immunity to the allure of Dawn, but I suspected that the longer we stayed, the more this place would affect us. The power of the White Wings was strong. This entity had managed to withstand it for over three weeks, and I was about to head into a building that housed this beast.

Michael stormed out of the lift, his face like thunder. "I told you to wait for Raguel."

Bane looked up from his glass of whiskey. "Yes. You did."

"Then why didn't you."

Bane downed his drink and stood, his powerful frame equaling Michael's. "Whose investigation is this?"

Michael's brow wrinkled. "The MPD's, of course. But we need to be kept informed about *everything* that occurs."

"And *we* need to be given the freedom to follow our instincts and chase leads as we see fit. If you're expecting us to wait around for a White Wing to be free to tag along, then this isn't going to work." Bane's tone was reasonable but brooked no argument.

Michael pinched the bridge of his nose. "Fine. What did you discover?"

Rivers filled him in on our visit in a

concise, economical manner.

Michael turned to me. "Well, Harker, it looks as if you have a focus for your investigation."

"And I'd like to get started."

He inclined his head. "Very well, come with me. I will introduce you to my harem, and they will prepare you for the bedding. Maybe you can get some information out of them during the process."

Oh, yeah. The bedding ceremony. "How long does this ceremony usually last?"

The corner of Michael's mouth lifted. "Usually, till dawn. But don't worry. I'm sure we can find something to keep us occupied."

"Michael …" Bane warned.

He laughed. "Card games usually work. Or chess. Do you know how to play chess?"

"Yeah, I do." I wasn't going to allow him to rile me up. "Let's just get this over with so I can do my job."

Leaving Orin, Rivers, and Bane behind, I stepped into the lift with Michael. For the next three days, I was on my own. For the next three days, it would be up to me to root out our primary suspects.

Michael and I strode up a flight of stairs marked *roof access*. "I'm going to need a list of everyone who has contact with your harem."

Michael glanced over his shoulder. "I can do that."

"And we need to talk about Caroline. I need you to tell me everything you know about her. Anything she may have said to you during your time together, anything you may have gleaned."

"I told you, I don't have that kind of relationship with my harem."

"Bullshit. You don't fuck someone regularly and not learn anything about them. You must have picked up on stuff, even subconsciously. So fucking think."

A small part of my brain whispered that I needed to back off, that speaking to a White Wing this way wasn't a wise move, but it was just a whisper, easily ignored.

"Damn, you have a foul mouth." He sounded excited by that.

Urgh. "I assume we'll be flying to our next destination."

"You assume correctly."

We exited onto the flat roof of the tower — the sky above and a sheer drop to the cement twenty stories below.

"Come here." Michael held out his arms.

Man, I'd have to touch the arrogant sod. I stepped into his embrace, and he wrapped his arms around me.

"Hold on, Miss Harker. Don't be shy."

"I'm a survivalist. So, trust me. I'll be holding on."

His grip tightened, and then we were shooting up into the air like a fucking rocket. White wings burst from his back, stretching wide and magnificent, and for a long, terrifyingly glorious second, we were suspended in the air, just gliding and arching toward the ground. I bit back a yelp.

And then his wings began to beat, catching the air and slowing our descent. I closed my eyes and tucked my head into the curve of his shoulder and ignored the arm cradling my butt.

Man, I hated flying.

We landed on a tidy green lawn. A two-story, flat-roofed building sat in the center. Two women were sitting on a blanket enjoying a picnic lunch. They scrambled to their feet, their faces lighting up at the sight of Michael, and then their dark gazes slid to me, and curiosity furrowed their brows.

"June, Karen, this is ..." He paused and glanced down at me.

He didn't know my first name. "Serenity."

"Yes, yes, Serenity. Take her and prepare her for the bedding ceremony, then bring her to the main house."

The main house? *This* wasn't the main house? I opened my mouth to question him, but he was already in flight. Great. The two women exchanged glances. They were both dark-haired beauties, probably in their early twenties.

"So, you're the first replacement," the curvier one said. She sounded ... disappointed.

Her companion nudged her and then plastered a smile on her face. "I'm June, and this is Karen. We're delighted to have you join us. Please, come this way."

She padded barefoot across the grass toward the boxy building. Everything here had a modern feel to it. Doors slid open on approach, and the temperature adjusted around my body so it wasn't too warm or too cold. The interior was minimalistic and an open plan: a low coffee table, several long sofas resembling chaise lounges, and a dining table at the far end of the room. It looked impersonal and uncomfortable.

June must have noticed my expression, because she said, "Don't worry, this is just where we entertain guests. We live through here."

Down a short corridor to the right and through a door into a large room filled with laughter and music and color. Cushions and rugs and a couple of swing seats, but mostly seating cushions on the floor, made up this space. A wave of contentment and euphoria washed over me, and both the women accompanying me sighed.

"Isn't it wonderful?" June said. "You are so lucky to be chosen."

I glanced at Karen, who smiled, but it didn't really reach her eyes. It seemed that this was one woman who wasn't so affected by whatever juice the White Wings were pumping into their air.

Several of the occupants of the room broke off their conversation to look over at us—three males and five females. They were all in their mid-twenties, and all dark-haired and brown-eyed. It looked like Michael had a type, a type which so wasn't me. With my auburn hair and blue eyes, I stood out like a sore thumb.

I raised a hand in greeting. "Hey. Good to be here."

One of the males, a bronze Adonis with abs to die for, stood up fluidly and ambled over. "Larson. Nice to meet you." He held out his hand and I shook it. "You'll be very happy here."

"I hope so."

He cocked his head. "Are you nervous about the bedding?"

June nudged me. "Larson is very empathic."

Really? I resisted the urge to roll my eyes and decided to just go with it. "Yes. I am. So nervous." I shivered for emphasis.

He smiled. "A virgin."

Like heck. But I lowered my lashes and nodded.

There were several awws and oohs from

the group, and suddenly everyone wanted to soothe my fears.

"A gentle lover."

"Considerate and kind."

"Won't rush things."

Phrases were thrown at me, and yes, this was good, because I had them talking. They had their guard down, all except Karen. She remained slightly apart, on edge and wary. My stomach clenched in warning. My gut told me that this was the woman I needed to get through to.

"Okay, okay," June said, waving everyone away. "We need to get Serenity ready for Michael. You'll all have time to get to know her tomorrow."

June took my hand and led me across the room, through another door and into a glass corridor spilling sunlight onto tiles. The corridor connected two parts of the house, and June led me into the second half. There was a dining area, a second lounge, and then two sets of stairs leading up to a balcony.

"This way," June said brightly.

Karen hung back to allow me to follow and then made up the rear. It felt like they were herding me, which was dumb, because it wasn't as if I had anywhere to run to even if I was inclined to do so. We passed several closed doors—bedrooms, no doubt—and stopped at the end of the corridor.

"This will be your room," June said. "I'll get some sheets to make up the bed while you're with Michael. It will be all ready for when you get back."

She pushed open the door, and we entered a sun-drenched room around the same size as my chamber at the mansion, but that was where the resemblance ended. This room was modern and chic and, like the rest of the house, minimal. A low dresser, a wardrobe, and a bed. That was it.

"Bathroom is through here." Karen led the way this time, pushing open the wall, which was a cleverly hidden door. Cool.

June hurried in and the sound of running water followed.

Karen wandered over to the wardrobe. "Go on, you can go into the bathroom, she won't bite." She smiled again, but once again, it didn't quite reach her eyes.

June looked up from swirling bubbles into my bath. "Is the temperature all right?"

I tested it with a hand. "Yeah. It's fine."

She turned off the taps and then sat back, waiting.

Okay, was she seriously going to just watch me undress? I unzipped the dress. She smiled politely. Looked like she was here for the long haul. Sod it. I kicked off my shoes and stepped out of the dress and straight into the bath. The heat singed my skin, hotter than my fingers had picked up, but like hell was I jumping back out.

"Would you like help bathing?" June asked.

Fucking hell, was she serious? "Erm, no thanks." I sank farther under the bubbles.

June's face fell in disappointment.

"Very well, just come down to the lounge when you're done," Karen said. "I've left a robe on the bed for you to wear when you see Michael." She was so ready to leave, which made me want her to stay even more.

"Wait. Some company would be nice."

Did Karen just roll her eyes?

June beamed and parked her butt on the edge of the bath. "Of course."

Karen's eyes narrowed. "So, how did you get chosen?"

Best to stick with the cover story. "I'm a tribute from Midnight."

Her eyes widened. "You lived in Midnight?"

I had her attention now. "Yes."

"What's it like?" June asked.

"Dangerous. Which is why more humans need to know about their options. They need to know that they can be safe in Dawn. I volunteered as tribute to the White Wings so they would consider opening the lines of communication between Dawn and Midnight." I was echoing Abbadon's words, and June was buying it, but Karen's face was impassive.

I wasn't meant to know about the murders, but maybe if I nudged then they might tell me.

"Midnight humans need to know that Dawn is the safest place in Arcadia. When there is death on every corner, a place where there is no violence or murder can be mighty alluring."

June's smile faltered, and she glanced at Karen, but Karen, the hard bitch, kept her expression neutral.

"Dawn is the safest place in Arcadia. And you're lucky to be here," Karen said smoothly.

June nodded enthusiastically.

Another wave of euphoria washed over me as a surge of well-being drifted in through the fucking vents in the wall. June simpered but Karen merely sat up straighter, her breathing shallow. The wave passed and she relaxed. Was she fighting it? Immune to it? No. Humans weren't immune, which meant … could she be infected with the entity?

June handed me a loafer. "Come on, lazy bones. We can't keep Michael waiting."

Damn it. I needed to know for sure, and the only way to do that was to get my hands on her. I'd have to get Karen alone.

The main house was accessed via another one of those nifty glass corridors, but the ladies didn't come in with me. They left me at the doors with reassurances and, in June's case, excited giggles.

All the hype had wound me into a knot, and for a few moments, I'd almost forgotten that none of this was real. I was not going to have to bed a White Wing. The door closed behind me with a snick, and it was like stepping into a different era, or a mixture of eras. Candelabras, wooden floors, roaring fire, brickwork walls, gothic arches, and sculpted balustrades made up this living space.

Michael padded barefoot into the room in loose-fitted pants and a cream T-shirt. His hair had been pulled off his face, and he looked relaxed and at ease. The robe Karen and June had put me in felt suddenly too flimsy under his regard. He had no right to be looking at me like that. Seriously? He was checking out my cleavage now? Urgh.

"Hey." I clicked my fingers. "Eyes on the face, please."

He chuckled. "I'm sorry. Your assets are distracting." But he did look away, so that was something. "Have they been treating you all right?" he asked.

"How could they not, when their lungs are being filled with goodwill."

He flashed his teeth. "You think that's bad?"

"I like my free will."

"And you have it."

"And so should they."

His eyes darkened in anger. "We are not here to discuss the fate of humanity. We're here to catch a murderer."

"To protect Dawn's image."

He inclined his head. "Exactly."

I snorted. "The humans don't matter to you at all, do they? Their deaths don't matter. You had sex with these women, and now they're dead. Doesn't that bother you?"

He took a menacing step toward me and then caught himself. "Yes, it bothers me. They belonged to me and someone killed them. They were meant to be safe in my care. I promised them that, and I was made a liar of. So, yes, it bothers me."

I deflated. What was the point? He just didn't get it. He cared about loss of face, loss of resources. He didn't care about the actual individuals who'd died. But then he wasn't human and, unlike me, didn't have even an ounce of humanity in him.

"Forget it."

"You're disappointed." He sounded taken aback.

Ten out of ten for observation. "It's not important. What is important is that I think I may know who our host is."

His body grew alert. "Already?"

I shrugged. "I can't be sure. Not until I get her alone. I'd need to touch her to know for sure."

He nodded slowly. "Who do you suspect?"

"Karen."

His brow furrowed. "Karen was one of the first. What makes you suspect her?"

It was on the tip of my tongue to tell him, but I bit back the words. If, by some long shot, Karen had built up an immunity to Dawn's influence, then it wouldn't be fair for me to out her for it. Who knew what the White Wings would do to a human immune to becoming silvered, and who knew how the Black Wings might use this knowledge to our advantage.

"Just a gut feeling. I could be wrong."

"Very well. What would you like to do to pass the time?"

He took a step closer, and his fresh, clean scent hit me, mingling with the essence of joy in the room to create a tugging and yearning inside me. His blue eyes twinkled knowingly.

I smiled thinly. "You said you had cards?"

He let out a bark of laughter. "Are you sure?"

I cocked my head. "Let's cut the crap. Even if I were up for some fun, I've seen your harem, remember—dark hair, dark-eyed—I'm hardly your type."

The twinkle in those pretty eyes dimmed. "I'll get the cards."

This yearning wasn't real. It was coaxed and elicited by the air of this place, and maybe a human would be fooled, like the poor delusional men and women in the harem. They thought they loved him, they thought they desired him, and maybe they did to a degree, but not to the level of devotion that I'd seen on their faces. All except Karen. Karen was here because she wanted to be. And it was up to me to find out if something else was in here with her.

My reception back at the harem the next morning was warm and filled with questions about my bedding. What could I say? I had a great sleep in the master bed while Michael took the armchair? Yeah, who knew that White Wings could be so chivalrous?

Coy Serenity came out to play, and they

soon stopped asking. The day passed lounging on cushions and listening to music. It was impossible to get Karen alone, and then she simply disappeared. June stuck by me, though, making sure the others didn't overwhelm me with their questions about Midnight. It did give me the chance to get to know them a little, although being silvered seemed to have stripped them of actual personality. Karen had to be the culprit, because it was impossible to imagine any of these simpering humans hosting an entity, and if they were, it would be an entity with fantastic acting ability.

We were finishing up our evening meal of roasted chicken and vegetables when one of the guys spoke up.

"Sarah would have loved this roast. It's cooked to perfection."

The room fell silent. This was my cue. "Who is Sarah?"

"Good one, Justin," one of the women said.

The guy, Justin, ducked his head. "I miss her, okay. It's not fair we can't talk about her."

For a moment, a solemn air fell over the gathered, and then another blast of that damned pixie dust floated into their lungs, and they were instantly all cheery again.

"But she's in a better place now," Justin said.

I arched a brow. "A better place than Dawn?"

The others all nodded. "Her soul is free. We should be happy for her."

"Rejoice."

A chill ran up my spine. Three women had been murdered, and instead of mourning, they were celebrating the fact they were dead? This was way too creepy for me.

"She died?" I injected a smidge of horror into my tone, not too much. If one of them was sporting the entity, it needed to think I was silvered like the rest. "How did she die?"

Once again, the mood dipped, as if my questions were cutting through the aura of well-being.

"They were murdered," Karen said from the doorway. She walked in and lowered herself onto a vacant cushion.

"They?"

"Three murders."

"Karen!" June admonished. "We agreed not to taint this place by speaking of what has happened."

Karen pressed her lips together. Various emotions I couldn't define flitted across her face, and then she sighed and nodded. "Of course. I'm sorry. I just miss them."

Didn't they wonder who the killer was? Wonder whether they were fraternizing with the murderer of their friends? Being silvered was totally fucked up.

Evening rolled around way too quickly,

and it was with a growing sense of frustration that I settled into my quarters. There'd be no sleep for me, though. I'd wait and then find Karen. If she had something to do with this, then I'd know soon enough. Michael wasn't far, and he'd summon Bane and the others. Damn. I missed the guys. At least the bed here was super comfy. Now to wait for the house to settle and go in search of Karen.

Minutes ticked by. Damn, this was boring. How long before everyone fell asleep? My door clicked open, and a figure entered.

I sat up. "Karen?" Well, this was a turn for the books. "What do you want?"

She closed the door. "I want to know who you really are and what you're doing here."

Okay, was not expecting that. My muscles were immediately alert, ready to fight if need be. If she was infected, then she could attack at any moment.

"I don't know what you mean."

"Yes, you do. You're a shit actress. You're just lucky the others are too doped up on Dawn joy to see it."

"Wow, that hurts."

She cracked a smile. "You're like me, aren't you?"

I held my breath.

"You're immune."

I'd been right about her. Or had I? Was this a trick? Shit, I was so confused. Think, Harker.

How to play this? Play along, of course.

"How long have you known?"

She shrugged. "Since I got here. Everyone was so ... happy. I wanted to be like them, just lose myself in this place, but it never happened. I realized divine joy has no effect on me. At first, I thought there was something wrong with me, like maybe I was evil or something. But then I thought, you know what, fuck it. This place isn't so bad, even if everyone is a moron."

"You seem to get on okay with June."

"I get on with everyone. It's what you do when you're silvered."

"Doesn't it get frustrating?"

She chuckled. "God, yes. Sometimes I have to walk away and just scream, then I come back and get on with it."

"What about leaving?"

Her smile dropped. "There is no leaving. You know that ... or do you?" She moved closer to the bed. "What are you really doing here, Serenity?"

She was perceptive, this one, and I led with my gut. "I'm here to investigate the murders."

She perched on the bottom of my bed. "I knew it. I knew that's why you were here. You're so not his type. But the others are too gone to see it."

"What can you tell me?"

"Not much. I've been wracking my brains over it, but the White Wings have been so hush-

hush about it, I wasn't sure what to do. I spoke to Michael, and he said they were working on it and not to worry, so I did my happy face and that was it. But I've noticed that some of the others have been having nightmares since the murders, even though they seem fine during the day."

"I guess Dawn mojo can't silver your subconscious ..." Wait, there was something there.

"What? What is it?" she asked.

"I'm not sure. Just that the murders all took place at night when the subconscious is most in control." There was a connection there, but pushing it wouldn't help. I'd let *my* subconscious deal with the problem. "Tell me about Caroline. Was she seeing anyone in the house?"

Karen licked her lips. "Not just one person. She was seeing three. After she died, it all came out. Justin, June, and Liam were all so upset they ended up speaking out, and then they realized she'd been sleeping with them all. I'm sure if everyone wasn't so silvered up there'd have been a blowout. But as it stood, they moved past it." Her brows flicked up. "You don't think one of them found out before she died and killed her out of jealousy do you?" She caught her bottom lip between her teeth. "No, that wouldn't make sense." she said, discounted her own theory. "There is no jealousy here. Well, not enough to lead to a crime of passion."

This would be my cue to fill her in on the entity. But that wasn't an option. It was top-level clearance stuff. It didn't stop me wanting to spill, though.

"What about visitors?"

"We don't get nighttime visitors here. Only Michael."

And I'd crossed the White Wing off, as he'd been the one to report this and bring it to us. Okay, that put us at square one with—

A scream sliced through the silence. Karen and I locked gazes, and then we both made for the door.

June sat up in bed, eyes dazed, her hands out in front of her. "No. No. No. Don't make me." I gripped Karen's arm to stop her barging into the room. Instead, we huddled in the doorway and watched.

June rubbed her hands and shook her head. "No. No. No. Stop it. I don't want this. I don't." And then her eyes rolled back in her head, and she flopped back onto the pillows.

I tiptoed into the room, my footsteps muted by the thick pile carpet, and came to a stop at the head of her bed. I needed to touch her, to check.

"What are you doing?" Karen whisper-hissed.

I held a finger to my lips and then turned back to June and carefully laid a hand on her forehead. She moaned in her sleep but didn't wake up. The aether rippled around me, speckled with golden motes of light. If there was something inside her, I'd feel it now. It would reveal itself. There was no disturbance in the aether. No tug alerting me to an alien presence.

June was clean.

Karen and I slipped from the room and I grabbed her wrist, slipping effortlessly into the aether again. I needed to be sure.

"What are you doing?" She tried to pull free.

"Hush." Her eyes were wide and slightly frightened, but there was no need to be. "You're clean."

"I don't understand."

"You don't need to. Just show me to the other rooms."

She grabbed my elbow. "Not until you explain what the heck you're doing."

Fuck it. I filled her in quickly, just the basics about an entity and the fact yours truly could root it out.

"So, that's why Michael brought you in."

"Yes. Now, help me."

This hadn't been part of the plan, but now that we were doing it I wondered why the heck it hadn't been my first call of action? I guess having backup in the form of a human immune to Dawn mojo helped.

Half an hour later, we'd scanned everyone, and my heart was pounding in my chest.

They were clean.

"They're all clean."

Karen blew out a breath. "Come on. A hot drink will help us think."

The kitchen was sleek and modern with no appliances on show, but Karen set to work with milk and a pan to make hot chocolate.

"What now?" she asked. "What does this mean?"

I perched on a stool. "I don't know. If the entity isn't here, then maybe it moved?"

"It can body jump?"

"We don't know. We know so little about it."

She moved out of my line of vision and cupboards opened and closed. "What do you know? What makes you so sure the killer is possessed by this entity anyway?"

"Because it would be impossible for a human to kill in Dawn, not while silvered. You said yourself. They're always content and happy but ..." A human not silvered could do whatever the fuck they wanted. Mother fu—

The cold tip of a blade pinched my throat.

"Finish your sentence, Serenity," Karen said.

"You killed them. Just you."

"Yeah, just me. Have you any idea how

fucking annoying they are? Always dancing and laughing and marveling at every little fucking thing. It's enough to drive you insane. I even began an affair with Caroline just to alleviate the boredom. She let me do what I wanted to her, and then that got boring too. I guess I snapped, and snapped again and again."

She was insane. Question was, had she been insane before coming to Dawn, or had Dawn driven her cuckoo, and did her immunity to Dawn mojo have something to do with her psychopathic tendencies. Damn it, none of that mattered if she slid that blade into my throat. It would be bye-bye, Harker.

"I didn't plan on killing you. Believe it or not, having you here may have made this place bearable." She sounded almost sad. "I thought you were immune like me, but you're not human, are you? You're a neph. I'd never have told you my secret if I'd suspected that, so well played there. You faked being human pretty well."

I'd had my fair share of practice, but now wasn't the time to brag. Pulse pounding against the blade edge, I took shallow breaths. "Karen. You don't have to kill me."

"Shut up." The knife dug in, nicking my skin with a burning sting. "I can't let you tell them about my immunity. They'll kill *me*."

She wasn't worried about being caught out for the murders. All she cared about was protecting her secret. There was no way out of this for me. Not without backup. Lucky for me, I carried some around at all times.

I dropped my shields.

My daimon surged to the surface, teeth bared and eager to protect. She'd been watching the show. The next move was lightning fast. Neph speed, baby. I had her wrist in an iron grip, and my daimon began to siphon.

Karen cried out in shock, and my daimon purred as pure white energy laced with purple and brown poured into me.

The knife slipped from Karen's grip and clattered to the floor. My daimon wanted more, but Karen was fading, and unlike her, I was not a murderer.

Enough.

My daimon let go, and the human fell to the floor, shoulders heaving.

"What did you do?" Her voice was a weak rasp.

"What I had to in order to survive."

She raised her head to look at me, her eyes twin pools of desperation. "So did I."

"I can't believe it," Michael said for the fourth time.

We stood at the gates to Dawn, ready to take our leave. I'd quashed the impulse to see Jesse, because if she was anything like the other silvered, then I didn't want to know. Best to remember her as she'd been.

"You need to look into this," Bane said. "If there are more humans with immunity to being silvered, then you need to address that, evict them. Dawn can be a paradise for those living life through rose-tinted spectacles, but to the immune, it could literally drive them insane."

"Or maybe she was already insane," Rivers said. "The immunity may have been as a direct result of a chemical imbalance in her brain."

But there was more to it than that. "What about the nightmares the others were having?" I looked from Rivers to Michael. "Could that be an after-effect of Dawn's mojo? Could it be affecting the humans' subconscious minds?"

Michael blew out a breath. "We'll take care of it. Now we know what to look for."

There had been no option but to tell the White Wings about the immunity. As much as I'd have liked to hold on to that information to give the Black Wing cause an upper hand, it was the only explanation for Karen's ability to murder.

How many more potential killers were living in Dawn? How long before they crawled out of the woodwork?

I leaned back against the van, my body begging for sleep. It was still night out, but once I'd handed Karen over to Michael, he'd insisted we leave under cover of night. Our short visit was over; there would be no seeing The Powers. This was something that I was sure they'd be sweeping under the carpet.

There was no entity in Dawn, and I just wanted to curl up in bed and sleep for a week.

Orin scooped me off my feet. "Come on, sleepy head. You can sleep on my lap in the car."

We may have solved Dawn's problem, but the entity was still out there, and something was still coming. Ambrosius's words surfaced in my mind. *The veil is thinning,* he'd said. *All will be revealed when the enemy is released. Soon, it will be time.* I needed to figure out what that meant. Oleander might have cracked the books by now… Yeah, I'd speak to … a yawn cracked my jaw.

Orin carefully lowered me into the car, climbed in after me, and then pulled me into his lap. His body was warm, hard, but soft in all the right places.

I curled into him and closed my eyes.

I woke wrapped in cozy warmth and tangled limbs. My head was cushioned against a taut chest, and the soft fabric of a dark T-shirt was pressed to my cheek. Soft snores drifted over my head. I knew this scent—sea air and salt. I'd fallen asleep in the car, and he must have carried me up here, laid me down, and fallen asleep with me. He'd slipped off my boots, but the cream dress was tangled around my thighs. Carefully extricating myself from his embrace, I sat up and looked down on Orin's sleeping form. His dark hair was mussed, and my fingers ached to run through the silken strands, but that would wake him, and then we'd be in bed together. Awake. He belonged to Cassie. He shouldn't be here. I brushed the tousled strands of dark hair off his forehead anyway, indulging in the sensation of silk against my fingers.

He moaned and opened his sleep-kissed eyes. He blinked, rising out of the depths of whatever dream he'd been swimming in, and his pupils dilated, drinking me in. He reached up to cup my cheek.

My door flew open and Cassie's wild-haired silhouette was framed in the light from the hallway.

"Orin?" She choked out the word as if it were a shard of glass.

Yes. He wasn't mine.

Orin dropped his hand and tucked in his chin, keeping his back to Cassie. "It's not what it looks like."

But the truth was clear in his tone — it could have been exactly what it looked like. Guilt gnawed at my insides with its tiny, hot claws. I didn't take what was already taken.

I climbed off the bed. "I need some air."

I brushed past Cassie and out of my room. The yearning on Orin's face when I'd withdrawn stabbed at my heart, but I couldn't be a part of his conflict. My own emotions were all over the place. I'd be the last person to make his love decisions for him, even though my fingers had itched to slam the door in Cassie's face.

Knowing what you needed and wanted, and accepting the facts, were two separate issues, and I was still working on bridging the gap. Orin had to make his own journey.

It was barely three a.m., and the household was asleep. There was one place in the mansion where the worries of the world could simply fall away. I pushed open the door and stepped onto the roost to find that Bane had had the same idea. He stood at the balcony, looking out—his favorite pose. His wings were out. Was he about to take off, or had he just returned?

He glanced over his shoulder. "You didn't sleep long."

"I guess my body took what it needed."

"Did it?" He arched a brow.

Was he referring to Orin in my bed? My stomach twisted into a knot. "It's not like that." I cleared my throat and ducked my head. "He's just explaining that to Cassie now."

Bane let out a low whistle. "Orin's problem is that he'd rather take the hits than hurt anyone." He smirked. "It'll be interesting to watch him maneuver his way out of this one."

"There's nothing to maneuver. He carried me to bed, and he fell asleep with me. Nothing happened."

Bane's wings tightened as he turned to me, his face in shadow. "You think sex is the most intimate act between a man and a woman?"

"What?"

"Lying holding the object of your desire can be just as fulfilling as burying your shaft in her. Believe me. Something happened."

Guilt surged up my throat like bile. "It wasn't intentional."

He cocked his head, darkness flitting across his feral face. "But you want it to be, don't you?"

"Yes." The word was an explosion of angry breath. "I want it to be, because I'm fucked up, okay."

Saying the words out loud was like removing a stack of bricks that had been sitting on my chest. I could finally breathe, but my hands were trembling. My eyes burned in their sockets because the words were out there now, and they couldn't be unsaid.

Bane's expression softened, and he strode toward me and gently gripped my upper arms. "It makes you a fucking cambion, Harker. It makes you a neph. We aren't human."

"I know. I just don't want to hurt anyone."

"I'm not a neph that likes to share what's mine, but if I want you, any part of you, then I know there's no other way." He ducked his head. "It took all my self-control not to tear you from Orin's arms earlier. When you went into the room with Rivers in Dawn to console him, every carnal thing you could be doing with him went through my mind. It's not going to be easy watching the others grow close to you, but I'm not willing to give you up."

Now this was all on me, not them. These were my issues. "I doubt they feel that way. Orin has Cassie. He cares about me, but he loves her, and Rivers just wants to keep me safe. And Ryker is my friend, nothing more." My words sounded like weak excuses.

He shook his head slightly, as if despairing of me.

I reached up and ran my fingers across his

sculpted jaw, the beginnings of stubble rasping against my fingertips. "I can't give you up, though. You're under my skin, in my blood." I stepped closer, reveling in the heat of him. "I don't know what I'm doing. I don't even know what this is, but I want it to last. I want to find out."

He wrapped an arm around my waist and cupped the back of my head. "Just let go and allow your daimon to guide you. She will protect you — body and soul. This isn't Sunset, and you aren't hurting anyone by feeling the way you do. We're grown men. We can make our own decisions."

The vise around my heart relaxed, and I leaned into him.

He pulled me against him. "But right now, you're with me. Right now, in this moment, you're mine." His violet eyes flashed.

There was that heat that always knocked the breath from my lungs and left me weak-kneed.

He smiled, exposing those sexy fangs of his. "Let's go visit the moon."

I held on tight as we shot up into the air. Okay, maybe I didn't hate flying so much, especially when Bane's arms were holding me.

We filed into the lounge for our weekly meeting. The week had flown by with the usual patrols, banter, and training for the human unit. They were getting better every day, but it was all a distraction. What we needed was to figure out what The Breed was up to, and why they were trying to take us out of the picture. We needed to know who these entities were and what their agenda was, and we needed to figure out where this veil Ambrosius had mentioned was.

Orin and Rivers took the sofa opposite Ryker and me, and Bane took up his usual spot by the hearth, drink in hand. His hair was still damp from the shower. So was mine. Our gazes tangled, and I bit back a smile. My body still throbbed from his attentions, and the power I'd siphoned buzzed in my veins. Being with him soothed the confusion. Being accepted by him made it easier to accept myself, but still, I'd avoided Ryker, Rivers, and Orin the past few days. If my growing feelings for them were real, then distance wouldn't kill them. Ryker slung an arm over my shoulder and leaned across to plant a kiss to the side of my head.

"Hello, stranger."

Hello, guilt. "Sorry."

He smiled. "Don't be."

"Ryker, you got a report?" Bane asked, interrupting the moment.

Ryker sat back and crossed a kick-the-shit-out-of-you boot over his knee. "It's quiet. Way too quiet, especially after the manic activity of the last few weeks. No deaths, no attacks. The sea dweller patrol has reported the same."

"No sign of The Breed," Orin said. "They've gone underground." He snorted. "Probably literally."

"It's almost as if they're waiting for something," Rivers said.

"The calm before the storm," Orin said softly.

But there was more. Stuff we'd pushed to the side until now, hoping that it would eventually become clear, but we needed to actively chase answers. Bane and I had agreed to not mention we knew what the piper was, because to do so would mean telling the others about Bane's relationship with the Black Wings. But there was no reason we couldn't work on the veil issue that Ambrosius had warned me about. My gut told me if we figured this out then all the pieces would fall into place.

"We need to find this veil." I'd mentioned it to Bane and Ryker, but Orin and Rivers were clueless. I filled them in about my dream, about how I was sure it had something to do with Ambrosius being silent.

"I don't like the sound of that." Rivers's eyes narrowed speculatively.

"Neither do I." Bane topped up a glass and handed it to me. "It sounds like this veil falling is somehow linked to you."

I sipped the malt whiskey and winced as it burned my throat on its way down. "Oleander is on the last notebook. I asked him about any mention of the veil. So far, Jonathan only talked about the boundary wards. But Oleander is keeping an eye out. If he doesn't find anything useful, then I'm going to The Order."

"Whoa!" Ryker sat forward. "Let's not be rash."

"I'm not being rash. Marika said she had information about the daggers. Ambrosius is linked to the daggers, and he's the one who delivered the warning about the veil. It's all connected, and they may be able to help. They have knowledge we don't. Maybe they can tell me what this veil is?" The guys were silent. "Maybe it's time we put our differences aside, because I have a feeling that whatever we're up against will probably want to squash us all."

"If you go, then I'm coming with you," Ryker said.

"Let's hope it doesn't come to that," Bane said.

Cassie walked into the room. Her face was still pale but she looked much better than she had a week ago. Another few days, and she'd be back to her usual space. She slid onto Orin's lap, even though there was space next to him on the sofa.

Orin made a surprised sound and then our gazes locked—his apologetic and mine guarded. We'd barely spoken since we'd technically slept together. He needed his space to work things out with Cassie, and from the cat-that-got-the-cream look on her face, it looked like things were going great.

"What did I miss?" Cassie asked. She slid her fingers through Orin's hair.

"The extra seat, it seems," Ryker said dryly.

Cassie pouted. "Orin, you don't mind. Do you, baby?"

Orin tore his gaze off me. "No. It's fine."

"So, what did I miss?" Cassie asked again. She let out a breathy laugh. "Not the weeks I wasn't myself, but what did I *just* miss?"

She was trying too hard, and my heart ached for her. Nothing that had happened was her fault. My attachment to her boyfriend wasn't her problem. This was all me, and I needed to get over it.

"Not much," Bane said. "I'll fill you in on the past few weeks later if you like."

"For now, we're pondering the gathering storm," Orin added. "You feeling anything?" he asked her.

Of course, with her banshee tendencies, she may have picked up on something we hadn't.

Cassie's smile slipped. "Not really. I mean, it's probably nothing, but I've been having these weird dreams." Her tone was suddenly less confident. "They probably don't mean anything, but after being host to that *thing* for so long, I figure they might actually be some kind of residual memory or something."

"Go on." Bane walked over to the wingback and sat down.

Cassie slipped off Orin's lap and sat forward in her seat, hands dangling off her knees. "It's nothing concrete, just flashes and images. There's this shimmering barrier, like a veil."

My pulse kicked up, and I glanced at Bane. His lips tightened, but he didn't take his eyes off Cassie.

"But there's something behind it," she continued. "Shapes and shadows I can't make out, and then there's this feeling ... excitement and anticipation. It's almost"—she ducked her head—"sexual."

"The veil." Bane was on his feet again. "This damned veil. If we could only pinpoint its location, then maybe we could figure out what the fuck it is."

"Did someone say veil?" Oleander said from the doorway. His golden hair was mussed, his eyes bloodshot, but his grin was a beautiful thing to behold.

It was my turn to leap to my feet. "You found something."

"Yes. The final notebook is a study of alternate realities. He talks about soft spots in time and space, and then he goes on to talk about pockets of reality, and it's all wonderful and science and magic and—"

"And the veil?" Bane said, impatient for

him to get to the point.

"Here." Oleander held out the book.

Bane rolled his eyes. "If I could read the damned books, I'd have gone through them myself."

Oleander snatched the book back. "Sorry, um … Here, it says that there are specific times every few years where the various veils between worlds become thin, and at this time, it's possible to cross over, or for things to cross into our world."

I shot Bane a sharp glance. "Ambrosius said the veil would come down."

Oleander shook his head. "No. Jonathan specifically claims that the veils can only be penetrated by powerful magic, and only a handful of times in a mortal century. It doesn't say anything about them coming down." He flipped a page. "He mentions The Order and something called Samhain. Apparently, The Order celebrate this event once a year, and they claim it is a time when the veil between the living and the dead is thin."

"And you think Ambrosius was referring to this veil?"

"I don't know." Oleander closed the book and held it to his chest. His gold-flecked gaze was pensive. "I suppose it could, or it could refer to another veil, or maybe this Samhain affects more than one veil."

I pulled my phone from my pocket and

scrolled for Marika's number. I'd saved it off the card she'd given me weeks ago.

Bane's shadow fell over me, his chest at my back. "What are you doing?"

"Calling Marika to arrange a meeting."

"Wait. Before you do that, there is one more thing we can try."

I threw up my hands. "I'm all ears."

"We can give Jonathan another visit."

"You think he's able to speak to us now?"

"We won't know until we try."

What did we have to lose but a little of our time? "Fine. But we go now, and if he can't help, then we reach out to The Order. Deal?"

"Deal."

"No," Doris said. "He's not ready. He's not himself."

"Is he coherent enough for a conversation or not?" Bane asked evenly.

Doris glanced over her shoulder at the mausoleum. "He's coherent but delicate."

Bane held out his hands, palms up. "Then I promise I will treat him as if he were made of fucking glass."

Doris rolled her eyes. "And there he is, the Bane I know. I was wondering when you'd show your claws."

Bane made a sound of exasperation. "You know I wouldn't be here if it wasn't important."

"Unfortunately, I do. But what's important to the living means nothing to the dead."

Bane's biceps flexed, a sure sign he was about to lose it.

I placed a hand on his arm. "This very well may affect the dead. Jonathan was researching the veils between our world and others, the veil between the living and the dead. We believe that something bad is about to happen. Something concerning one of those veils, and we're hoping that Jonathan can help fill in the gaps in our knowledge."

Doris placed a hand on her hip and slid a flat look Bane's way. "Next time, let her do the talking."

Bane growled low in his chest.

"And you can knock that out too." She turned away. "I'll bring him out, but do not mention anything about his death. He knows he's dead, but dwelling on the way he died could undo him."

She ducked into the mausoleum, leaving us to the starry night and dancing fireflies.

I tapped my fingers on my thigh. "Well, that went well."

Bane made a harrumph sound.

"What's wrong with you? You've been in a shitty mood ever since we left the mansion."

He pinched the bridge of his nose. "I don't know. I just have this feeling that everything is about to change, that we're moving toward a conclusion that is also a beginning. It's in the air, like the electricity before a storm." His mighty shoulders heaved. "I wouldn't normally give a crap. Fighting bad shit is what I do, but ..." He locked gazes with me. "But now ... Fucking hell, Harker. Now I have you."

He was afraid ... afraid of failing, of not figuring this out on time. My throat tightened. "Nothing is going to happen to me. We're going to figure this out." I wrapped my arms around him and inhaled him. "Whatever comes, we'll fight it. Together."

He stroked my hair with his huge hand, running his palm down my back and resting on the dip in my waist and the rise on my buttocks.

"Recently, the only time this feeling goes away is when I'm inside you."

My stomach clenched and my core tightened. "Well, at least I know how to make you feel better," I teased.

He chuckled into my hair. "That you do."

Movement in the mausoleum caught my eye. Bane released me as Doris returned, arm linked with a tall, graying man.

"Jonathan." Bane took a step forward, but Doris held up her hand to ward him off.

Bane stepped back and tucked his hands into his jeans pockets. His pose was relaxed, unthreatening, but I knew him well enough to know that the neph was always on high alert.

"It's good to see you, Bane," Jonathan said.

His smile was watery. "I wish it was in better circumstances."

"So do I, my friend," Bane said. "I wouldn't be disturbing you so soon, but we need your help."

He shook his head. "No. I can't do anything. Not anymore. I did what I could."

The note and his books ... was that what he was talking about? Doris gave us a warning look.

Bane exhaled sharply through his nose. "Yes. What you left us has been very helpful. We went through your books. You talk about veils. We believe one is about to come down. Do you know where it is? What it leads to?"

Jonathan squeezed his eyes shut. "It was in my head. It was there all the time, but I fought it and then it fought back. It called the ripper, and it killed me." His eyes widened and glazed over, as if he was recalling that very moment. "It ripped out my heart. My heart. I have no heart."

His face drained of all color, and he clutched at his chest. Doris shot us a lethal look and pulled him back toward the mausoleum. The door closed behind them, cutting off the music.

I guess our time with Jonathan was up. We weren't going to be getting any help from our dead friend.

Jonathan's words resonated inside my head. "He said something was inside him, in his head. Do you think it was one of those entities?"

Bane gripped the nearest tombstone, his jaw rigid. "I think it's time you called Marika."

I dialed, hyperaware of the tension radiating off Bane's body. It brushed against mine, communicating his anxiety. The phone rang for ages, and just as I was about to hang up, it was answered with a click.

"Hello, Marika's phone." The voice was male, with the residue of recent laughter clinging to it. "How can I help you?"

"Can I speak to Marika, please?"

"I'm afraid she's unavailable right now. Can I take a message?"

Who was this guy? Her personal secretary? "Yeah, tell her Harker called, and I'm ready for that chat."

Silence on the other end. "Miss Serenity Harker? From the MPD?"

"The one and only. And you are?"

"Frederick Blunt. I run The Order, Miss Harker. Marika is away on Order business at the moment, but I'd be happy to answer any questions you may have."

"When?"

"Tomorrow evening. Six p.m.?"

"Where?"

"I'm sure your colleagues are familiar with our address. Oh, feel free to bring a friend. We have nothing to hide." There it was again, that hint of humor.

I hung up. "Well, hopefully by this time tomorrow we'll have some answers."

I pulled the tray out of the oven and stared at the half-blackened lumps of dough. Great, just fucking great. Ryker and I would be leaving for our meeting with Frederick in a couple of hours, and I needed scones so bad right now. My stomach was queasy with nerves, and Orin's baked goods always soothed me, but there was no way I'd be asking him to bake them for me. Fucked up, really, because a week or so ago, I'd have had no problem waltzing into his room and yanking off his duvet and asking him to cook for me. But that was before the butterflies had spawned to life in my stomach around Orin. That was before Cassie had returned and killed them with her presence.

Best to stay away until this feeling went away.

Bootfalls alerted me to company.

"What's burning?" Orin appeared in the doorway.

I flipped open the bin and dumped the scones, but not before Orin saw them.

"Serenity?"

"It's nothing."

He arched a brow. "Looked like burned scones to me."

I winced.

"Why didn't you ask me?"

"It's not important. Honestly."

He walked over to the counter and surveyed the mess with hands on hips, his huge body taking up space, his aura brushing against mine.

"I'll clean it up." My mouth was dry. Dammit. Leaving wasn't an option, because the mess was mine, but standing here, with his scent surrounding me, was too much. "I'll clean it later."

I took a step, but his hand closed around my arm.

"I thought we were friends?" he said in a hushed voice.

Looking up at him would hurt, but if I was going to be convincing then that was what needed to be done. "We are friends."

His eyes narrowed. "Then why have you been avoiding me, Serenity?" His tone was soft, hesitant.

I tore my gaze from his. "I wanted to give you time with Cassie."

His fingers were warm and solid on my

arm. "Just because Cassie's back doesn't mean that we can't hang out." His voice dropped. "I miss you."

Oh, God. Why was he doing this? I smiled brightly, maybe too brightly. "I miss you too."

His focus dropped to my lips, but it was a brief caress, and he quickly shifted his attention back up to my eyes.

He released me. "So, it's settled. No more avoiding."

I nodded. "Deal."

"Now roll up your sleeves because I'm going to show you how to make proper scones."

I wasn't sure what I was expecting The Order headquarters to look like, but it certainly wasn't a tower block apartment building. Graffiti decorated the outside, colorful and explicit. Yeah, some people had a lot to say about The Order. Ryker buzzed the intercom, and we waited on the grimy steps.

"Seriously? This is their base of operations?"

Ryker nodded. "And where they live."

Crap. Like literally crap. It looked like dogs liked to dump the contents of their intestines around here too.

I covered my nose and mouth. "Damn, it stinks."

"Breathe through your mouth."

"But then I'll be *tasting* it."

He rolled his eyes but smiled. "Always with the retorts."

"And you love me for it."

His expression sobered, and my heart stuttered as something forbidden and forgotten skittered across the outer edges of my mind.

The intercom buzzed. "Yes?" the voice snapped. "What do you want?"

"We're here by invite to see Frederick," Ryker snapped back. His brow furrowed. "I fucking hate rude people." He said it with his finger on the button, loud enough for the speaker to hear, before releasing it.

"Floor Thirteen. Room 1309."

The door buzzed and popped, and Ryker pushed it open, leading the way. The foyer was just as bad as the outside, but at least the smell of shit was muted. I headed for the lift, but Ryker grabbed my arm.

"What?"

"We take the stairs."

Shit, of course. In a lift, we were penned in. They could stop it and leave us stranded, or be waiting to ambush us on the thirteenth floor. Stairs it was. My glutes needed a workout anyway, and Ryker's arse was the perfect distraction from my burning thighs.

We hit the thirteenth floor barely winded, and exited the stairwell onto the main corridor. Okay, this was slightly better. Clean floors, clean walls, and no excrement. Nice. Room 1309 was a black door, while all the rest had been white — a sign that this housed the big man, the don, the chief? Or maybe they just ran out of white doors? Who knows?

"Are you inner monologuing again?" Ryker asked.

"No."

He grinned. "Yes, you are. You get that little pucker just here." He fingered the spot between my brows. "And your lips go all pouty."

He'd been staring at my lips? "You observe way too much."

His blue eyes, made even bluer by the navy T-shirt he was wearing tonight, crinkled. "It's a curse."

I raised a fist to knock, but the door swung open unprompted. A plump man dressed in an ill-fitted suit with a bad dye job on his thinning hair greeted us. "Miss Harker and friend, I presume. Please, do come in."

I noted his ink-stained fingers and the nicotine patches on his nails. A writer who enjoyed smoking a lot? We followed him into the flat — open plan, clean, smelled nice. Ooh, there was even potpourri on the table. The curtains were closed to the moon, and the place was bathed in artificial light.

"Please, follow me." Frederick led us into a small office and closed the door. "Please, sit." He indicated the two chairs on the client side of his desk before dropping into the one at the business end. He slapped a hand on the wood and grinned, showcasing blunt, yellow teeth.

This was the leader of The Order? This unassuming, portly, nicotine-stained, balding, yellow-toothed man?

"Well, it's good to finally meet the infamous dagger carrier," Frederick said.

My hand went to my wrist covered by my long-sleeved polo shirt. He tracked the movement, his grin widening. "May I see?"

I shrugged, feigning nonchalance, even though some primal part of my brain had issued an alert. "Sure, when you've answered a few of our questions."

He raised a bushy brow. "Of course." He spread his hands. "What do you want to know?"

"I want to know about the veil."

He blinked, his smile falling. "The veil?"

"Samhain, or whatever you call it. When the veil between worlds is thinnest?"

His smile was back in place. "Ah, Samhain or All Hallows' Eve. Yes, yes. The Order does hold vigil on this night. Light candles and place them in pumpkins to trap the spirits that may wish to do harm. It's all harmless fun. Old tradition. Nothing to be concerned about."

That couldn't be right. There had to be more to it than that. "And could this veil fall?"

He let out a bark. "Fall? The veil between

life and death?" He shook his head. "No."

I exchanged looks with Ryker. Ambrosius had said that the veil was about to come down and then all would be revealed. If my daimon hadn't reiterated the words to me, and if Cassie hadn't mentioned a veil in her dream, then in the face of Frederick's flippancy, I'd have maybe fobbed it off as a figment of my subconscious.

"Okay, my turn." Frederick rubbed his hands together. "Let's see the daggers."

There was no way I was getting the actual blades out for him. Instead, I pulled up my sleeves and flashed the ink.

"Pretty, very pretty," he said. "I do wonder why they chose you, though. That is something I'm unsure of."

No point rising to the jibe. "Marika said you knew what they were. What they were for?"

He nodded sagely. "Oh, yes. They were left behind by Merlin when he sacrificed himself to strengthen the veil beyond this world and another. You see, Merlin had a gift, the gift of premonition and foresight, and he dreamt that a time would come when the veil would fall and this world would be overrun by its superiors."

"Wait, I thought you said the veil couldn't fall."

"I said the veil between the living and dead wouldn't fall."

A prickle of apprehension skimmed across my scalp and that primal warning intensified.

"Superiors?" Ryker asked. "You said overrun by superiors?"

Frederick arched a brow. "Oh yes. You aren't the first to taint this earth, but you'll certainly be the last."

Adrenaline flooded my veins. This was wrong, all wrong. "What are you talking about?"

Frederick sat forward. "I'm talking about those pretty daggers that can cut through anything. I'm talking about the fact that we thought we needed you to free our brethren, to make the cut that would allow them to walk the earth once more." He stood tall. "But we don't need you anymore. The veil is weak — barely a gauze barrier now. Ten more human souls, and we will be free. However, having a plan B always helps. And you, neph, are our plan B."

Ryker was on his feet, weapon in hand, before I could blink, before I could dip into the aether and see Frederick's true face. Darkness shifted beneath his skin, and crimson eyes glared back at me.

I rose steadily to my feet, my hands itching to release my only weapon, but I held off. "You're one of them."

"And you're the one who's been expelling my people." He opened his desk drawer and retrieved a gas mask. He held it to his face. "Don't worry. We'll make sure you get to see the show."

Ryker lunged at him as a hiss filled the

room, but then changed his mind, reaching for me instead.

"Venom!" He held me close.

My skin tingled and then the tainted air was being pushed away and circulated back toward the vents in the wall. Ryker was using his elemental power to try and keep the venom away from us.

"Nice trick," Frederick said. "But how long can you keep it up?"

They were pumping the room with the shit, and the air was suddenly thick and cloying with Arachne's venom. The same venom The Breed had used on me and Drayton. How had The Order got hold of it? They were working with them ... in on it together. Ryker coughed. Darkness inched in, claiming my vision. They were working together...

"Damn, hangover."

"You're okay," Ryker said. His face swam into focus, his brows furrowed in concern. "I think it's out of your system now."

I sat up, hands scraping against stone. Shit, where the heck were we? Gray and dank and yep, a cell. I fucking hated cells. Glass ones, barred ones, and ones made of stone.

Hated.

Ryker brushed back my hair and then

helped me to sit up against the wall. "I don't think we're in the tower block anymore."

"We're not," a familiar voice said.

I looked over Ryker's shoulder to find Marika watching from the shadows. She was curled up against the wall, her expression part sour, part defiant. I needed to sit forward, but, shit, my hands were tied behind my back. Great! There was no way I could get out of this one without the use of my daggers, and they'd be impossible to wield with my hands crossed and tied behind my back.

I shuffled back on my butt to brace myself better against the stone. "Okay, what the fuck is going on?"

"I only just came to and found we weren't alone." Ryker sat back on his haunches and looked to Marika. "Care to fill us in?"

Marika pressed her head back against the wall. "What's the point, we're all going to die anyway."

"Humor us," Ryker said.

"Frederick isn't Frederick anymore, and everything I thought we were working toward is a lie."

"What do you mean?"

"I mean that for the last several decades we've worked to try and find a way to bring Merlin back. We got wind of the daggers' existence a while back, and the hunch that the MPD may have them. It took a hell of a lot of power, but we managed to animate a golem to test the MPD wards and boundaries."

"Yeah, we know," Ryker said dryly.

She winced. "I'm sorry. It was meant to be barely a foot high. Just something to test your security. The plan had been to sneak in and scope out the mansion, but things went wrong and we lost control of the damned thing."

Well, that explained the crazy eight-foot clay monster we'd had to battle.

"We've always just wanted to put humans back in the driver's seat by getting rid of the angels' influence. Merlin had the weapons that could kill the angels."

"Black Wings," I corrected. "The weapons to kill the Black Wings."

She rolled her eyes. "Black Wings, White Wings, same thing. The weapons can kill both."

Damn it, of course they could. Black Wings had been White Wings at one time, after all. "So, you wanted to kill the winged?"

"No, we just wanted leverage. Threaten them to leave humanity alone, to lower the barrier keeping us trapped here and basically fuck off."

Sounded like a good plan.

"But things have been off for a while now," Marika said. "It started when our leader, Chris, just vanished, and Frederick took over. He started to make changes, shifting the hierarchy, promoting members to positions they really weren't suited to, and then it was all about the secret meetings and the recruitment drive. He even sent us to Sunset to try and bag more humans to join the cause. I told myself he was passionate about the rising, but I wasn't the only one noticing the changes in The Order—this imperceptible darkness that suddenly seemed to sit over everything. A few members were talking about leaving, so I went to speak to Frederick. I thought, hey, maybe he can do a speech or something to put everybody's mind at rest, even mine. And that's when I found out the truth." She paused to look directly at us, her slanted eyes flashing in the gloom. "Frederick had Chris murdered. He made it look like a neph attack. He's probably a John Doe somewhere." Her eyes welled, and she dashed away the tears.

I looked to Ryker. "The cold case Bane gave me was a John Doe that looked like a kelpie or something had taken chunks out of him."

Marika made a choked sound. "Oh, God."

"Why is he doing this?" Ryker asked. "What is his agenda?"

"Well, he doesn't give a shit about Merlin, that's for sure. All he cares about is the entity Merlin will be hosting. He called it Asher. From what I gathered, this thing is some kind of commander, and when the veil falls, he'll be stepping through with his army of shades. There are several shades already amongst us, ones that have been trapped on this side of the veil for some time—ones that managed to slip through the cracks over the years. The others that are due to come through will need hosts, though, and Frederick has been collecting humans."

The pieces were falling together in my mind. "The human recruitment. You guys recruited at the fete a few weeks back." It had been weird the way the humans had just upped and followed them. "You had a huge number of humans follow your disciple."

Her jaw clenched. "They've been working with The Breed, controlling the scourge and killing to weaken the veil. Human sacrifice is the key, apparently. The fete recruitment happened after Frederick had a visit from Maximilian."

"How could you be okay with working with The Breed? They kill humans, the humans you want to save."

"We weren't, we aren't. That's just it. But anyone who could do anything to object had been replaced by someone willing to go with the alliance."

"Order members infected with these shades?"

"I believe so. I've had a few days to think things through, and I believe that some of these shades must have gotten free somehow, or maybe they've always been among us. I don't know. But they can't do anything, not really, not without this Asher dude. The Breed and scourge spilled the blood, and somehow helped us recruit humans."

Ryker sat forward. "Serenity, what if they used bliss?"

Marika looked from me to Ryker. "What is that?"

"Kelpies produce it. It lulls their prey into a false state of euphoria." I shifted uncomfortably against the cold wall. "The Breed kidnapped a few kelpies to extract the hormone. We stumbled across it when we … when we lost Drayton."

Her expression softened. "I heard about that. I'm so sorry for your loss."

"We need to get out of here and warn people."

"Yeah. That had been my plan too until I got fucking caught." She snorted in disgust, probably at the fact she'd been captured. "I have no idea how many of The Order have been turned. But it's enough to take control, and the others don't have a fucking clue. It's Samhain, and Frederick is going to use the powers that thin the veils between worlds to make the final break. The Order thinks Merlin will rise tonight. There's a celebration planned. But instead, we'll be releasing some pre-winged race called the shades."

"Tonight? How long do we have?" I'd lost all concept of time.

"An hour, maybe less."

Ryker clenched and unclenched his fist. "The venom has fucked with my affinity. I can't seem to connect to the air."

"It's all right. We'll figure something out."

A key scraped in the lock and then the door was tugged open to reveal three built guys toting guns. Well, there was no outrunning a bullet. Ryker tucked in his chin. He was considering rushing them.

I nudged him with my shoulder. "Don't."

His fists clenched.

The gun was aimed at me. "Up."

Ryker helped me to stand.

"Out of the cell. Now."

Ryker walked forward and Marika stood up too. The man swung the barrel of his gun toward her. "Not you. You get back on the ground."

Marika slid back down, her jaw clenched.

The man smirked. "You'll be allowed out once it's all over. As for you two, you get the best seats in the house, courtesy of Frederick. He feels awful about the venom. He wants to make it up to you with the truth."

"We already know the truth," Ryker said through gritted teeth.

The gun-toting guy side-eyed Marika. "No. You only have half the story."

"Why do you care what we think?"

His eyes narrowed. "Because soon, you'll be forced to pick sides, and for your sake, let's hope you pick the right one."

They wanted to recruit us? What the fuck?

Ryker led the way out of the cell, and the door clanged shut behind us. I stumbled forward into Ryker's solid back. He turned and grabbed hold of my elbow.

I caught the gun guy's eye. "This would go a lot easier if you untied my hands."

"Just move." He waved his gun, ushering us forward.

Two guys ahead and one behind, we made our way through stone corridors, up a flight of steps, and onto a balcony overlooking a vast chamber.

How long had we been gone? Surely the others would be worried by now. They'd be looking for us. They'd go to the headquarters and take things from there. But hope didn't flutter, because hope knew that it was highly unlikely they'd find us in time to stop Frederick concluding his plan.

The man in question greeted us from the opposite balcony with the raising of a glass. Below us was an elaborate chalk circle covered in arcane symbols. And to the right stood the members of The Order, robed up, faces alight with excitement. A barrier had been erected to keep them away from the circle. They thought they'd be greeting Merlin, the savior of humanity.

The gun guy tucked his weapon away and stood, hands crossed in front of his crotch in classic bodyguard pose. The other two flanked us. Frederick raised his hand and The Order simmered down, eager to hear what their leader had to say. I scanned their faces and picked out the anxious, the wary, and the suspicious. Marika had been right. There were plenty of people who didn't trust Frederick.

"My brothers and sisters," Frederick began. "Today is a most auspicious day. Today is the beginning of a new era."

The arcane symbols began to glow softly, and a sigh went up.

"Yes. Yes. It is almost time. The veil is thin, the time is now, but in order to free the captive, we must make two sacrifices."

More members of The Order strode into the chamber. They were dressed in jeans and shirts, and like the guys holding us hostage, they carried guns. The Order members broke into a cacophony of exclamations and demands to know what was going on.

"Silence!" Frederick ordered. "You'll get what you want. You will get your Merlin. We are thankful to him, for his name provided us with a way into The Order. And his body provides our commander with a host, just like your bodies will eventually provide my fellow soldiers with hosts and you will have your savior. But for now ..."

The right side of the room filled with humans. Gaunt, dazed humans. Frederick's henchmen picked out ten, seemingly at random, and ushered them to the edge of the circle.

Ryker stepped forward and gripped the balcony. "Harker, I have a bad feeling about this."

"Understatement."

"No, I think they're going to—"

Gunfire filled the chamber and screams rose up to echo off the stone walls. I leapt forward, forgetting about my bound hands, and slammed into the balcony wall. Ten humans lay on the ground, their blood soaking into the floor and running in rivulets into the arcane circle. He'd killed them. He'd killed them in cold blood and The Order was going wild. Another round of shots and silence reigned. A jackrabbit took up residence in the pulse at my throat. How was the blood moving with such purpose, almost as if it was being attracted to the circle. It didn't make sense. All this death didn't make sense.

"Motherfucker." Ryker stumbled back.

Tearing my gaze from the carnage, from the suddenly neon-bright symbols, I looked up at Ryker's chiseled face, but his attention was elsewhere. I tracked his gaze to the opposite balcony and my heart did a somersault right into my throat.

A man stood next to Frederick. Tall and broad, his dark hair tousled in that sexy way that looked as if he'd just rolled out of bed. His chocolate-brown eyes lifted to lock with mine, and in that moment there was no death, no blood, and no evil mastermind about to take over the fucking world. In that moment, there was only Drayton, and my soul was crying once again.

The lock on my tongue broke. "Drayton!"

I pushed against the balcony walls. Frederick had Drayton. How the fuck? Oh, God. The Breed. They must have taken him hostage, and now he was here.

Drayton's brow furrowed as if he was puzzling over something, and then he leaned down to speak to Frederick. The shorter man smiled and nodded and said something back, and then Drayton straightened, his familiar lips curling in a smug smile.

Ice filled my veins. No. It couldn't be. He couldn't be one of them.

"Do it, Harker," Ryker said. "We need to know."

Stomach quivering, hands blocks of ice, I slipped into aether-sight. Drayton's handsome face blurred, darkened, and shifted, and his eyes flashed crimson.

"Well?" Ryker demanded.

"Not Drayton." Not anymore. But... "He could be in there. He could be trapped like Cassie."

The ground below us shuddered, the room rumbled, and then the circle dropped away to reveal a shimmering blue abyss.

The veil.

It was happening.

The veil was opening.

The blue began to darken, turning into a whirlpool, but then the swirl began to lose momentum.

"No." Frederick rushed forward. His head whipped up toward our balcony. "Bring them!" he ordered. "It's time for plan B."

I fell to my knees on the outer edge of the sluggish whirlpool. Frederick stood on the opposite side of the phenomenon. Ryker shrugged off his guards and earned the butt of a gun to his forehead for his efforts. He stumbled back with a grunt, his face contorted in suppressed rage.

"Leave him alone!" Damn these ties.

"Cut her free," Frederick said. "Try anything, and your lover's brains will be eating a bullet."

Shit. They had Ryker on his knees beside me, the gun pressed to his temple. A slight breeze ruffled my hair. Ryker made a sound of exasperation. Dammit, his affinity was still down. How the heck had mine come online so quickly? It didn't matter, there had to be something I could do. Some way to use the aether.

One of Frederick's minions cut my ties. I

rubbed my tender wrists. "What do you want from me?"

A slow smile spread across Frederick's face. "I want you to cut through the veil."

My daggers. They wanted me to use the daggers. Was that why Merlin had created them?

No ... I know now.

Ambrosius?

Frederick showcased his yellow teeth. "The veil would usually be immune to even the daggers' magic, but it is weak, thin enough to slice through. The time is now, Miss Harker. Liberate us or your lover dies."

"Don't," Ryker said.

Another hit to the head. He blinked, dazed this time. My body stiffened under the command not to attack the damned guard.

I glared at his attacker. "Touch him again and you die."

"Harker. One life to save the many," Ryker said.

"Don't listen to him." Drayton's smooth, dulcet tones assaulted my ears.

The world went still as I closed my eyes to ground myself. To remind myself that he was no longer Drayton. I couldn't look at him, didn't want to see the monster behind his pretty eyes.

"Look at me, Serenity?" he coaxed.

Oh, God. It sounded like him. Was it him? Was he in there? I slowly raised my lashes and met his steady gaze.

He hitched up his pants and crouched opposite me, beyond the swirling miasma of blues waiting to be split in two by my blade. The hues painted his skin in shades of indigo and turquoise, casting sharp shadows against his cheekbones and beneath his eyes.

"You made the wrong decision once," the thing in Drayton said. "You let me die. You plunged those daggers into me, and you watched the light leave my eyes." A ghost of a smile played on his lips.

He was mocking me. Playing with my emotions.

"You're not him. You're not Drayton."

His smile was cocky. "No. I'm just wearing him like a pretty suit, but I know things." He tapped his temple. "I know what you did, and I can guess how much you regret it." He jerked his head in Ryker's direction. "Do you really want to go through that again?" He cocked his head. "Make the cut, Serenity. Trust me, no one has to die today."

"No, they'll just be taken over by whatever comes through," Ryker spat.

Drayton's dark eyes glinted. "They'll be doing this world a service. We are the first, the superior race, and this world belongs to us." He stood up. "I promise you that humanity will be protected. Our grievance is not with mankind, but necessary sacrifices must be made to obtain our goal, and if you wish, you may fight alongside us."

"And what *is* that goal?" Ryker asked.

Drayton's smile was cruelly determined. "The annihilation of God and his precious winged."

My heart stuttered. "You want to kill the White Wings?"

"God must account for his sins, and all winged must die."

They didn't know that God was gone. Maybe they hadn't been able to take over a winged body to find out that bit of information. Neither revelation would matter if we didn't make it out of here alive. No deaths. Just bodies being taken over ... not deaths.

"Make up your mind, Serenity," the thing in Drayton's body said.

I searched his face. "Is he in there?"

Drayton blinked. "What?"

I needed to know for sure. "Is a part of him still alive?"

His lips parted, as if on a sigh, and for a moment he was unguarded, open. In that moment he was Drayton, and then the shutters came down and his lips thinned.

"You killed him, Miss Harker. There is nothing left."

Lying. He was lying. My heart was pounding so hard in my chest I was sure the world could hear it. The daggers appeared in my hands.

"Harker, no," Ryker warned.

I glanced over my shoulder. "No more death today, Ryker."

The humans taken by whatever came through could be saved. We'd find a way to save them. Drayton could be saved. I was not losing Ryker.

I slammed the daggers into the veil. For a moment, there was absolute pin-drop silence, and then the ground began to tremble and groan. White light shot up out of the whirlpool, blinding and glorious.

Serenity, I know. I know what I am, what you must do.

Ambrosius. I'm sorry. I had no choice. I can't let them hurt Ryker.

He is coming. I am coming. You must not let him have me.

I don't understand.

But a figure was stepping out of the light, a mighty warrior with raven-dark hair and winged brows. His body was wrapped in blue robes and wreathed in shadow. His penetrating gaze took in the scene. Several Order members fell to their knees, and Merlin's name was a mantra filling the room.

"Commander Asher," the guy with the gun said.

His companion repeated the words, and then the mantra changed and the new name took over.

Asher.

Serenity ... please.

Frederick rushed over to Asher and inclined his head in reverence. "Commander, you are free."

Asher's lip curled in derision. "Free but not whole. This soul was not complete. This body is not fully mine, you must find ..." He trailed off as his gaze fell on me. He canted his head. "What *is* this ..." He wasn't looking *at* me. He was looking *through* me. Shapes hovered at his back, dark shadows patiently waiting.

Serenity. Don't let him take me.

My chest began to burn with a strange tugging.

Asher slapped a hand to his chest, his brows snapping down. And then he threw back his head and laughed.

"Xavier," he said to Drayton. "You are truly a most loyal general. You have retrieved what was lost, and now I will claim it, and with it, the final vestiges of the power residing in this form."

Confusion flared in Drayton's eyes, but Asher was too busy devouring me with his gaze.

I'm gone, Ambrosius said. *He has devoured the rest of me. I am all that is left. Do not let him have me.*

"Commander. This is the neph the daggers chose," Frederick said. "She is also the neph who expelled two of our own from their human hosts. I believe she commands aether."

Asher's eye twitched. "This won't do. Not at all. I will retrieve what I need from her and then she must die."

His words barely registered because my mind was on a different track, making different connections. Merlin was gone. Asher had burned through his soul, but not all of it. It finally made sense. Ambrosius *was* Merlin. The final piece of the great wizard's soul, and without him, Asher wouldn't be fully in control of Merlin's power.

Serenity.

I scrambled to my feet and backed away from the circle, from Asher. I had to get out of here, away from him, but Ryker was still under guard, the gun to his head.

Asher held out his hand. "Give it to me."

The tugging intensified, like serious heartburn. "No."

His rugged face contorted in anger. "Give it to me. Now."

The pain flared like an inferno burning through my lungs and eating its way to my heart. My knees gave way, and I hit the ground, writhing in agony as every nerve ending lit up in anguish.

"Harker. Dammit, Harker!" Ryker was about to break. No. He couldn't. They'd shoot … Damn, it hurt.

A scuffle was followed by a muffled curse.

"Let the male neph go," Drayton said. "Tell her to give Asher the soul."

And then Ryker was by my side, pulling me into his lap, his hands all over me, trying to find the source of the pain.

"Tell her to stop fighting it," Drayton said.

But it wasn't me who was fighting. It was Ambrosius. He was fighting for his existence, and I needed to help him. My body bucked, and a slender, glowing white rope curled out of my chest and shot toward Asher. It slammed into him, and his eyes rolled in ecstasy.

"Yes! Come to me. This is where you belong." Asher held out his arms as if in greeting. "Fate has blessed us."

Serenity, I can't. I can't hold on.

This wasn't right. Why would Merlin leave a part of his soul behind to stop Asher getting hold of it when it was going to be so easy for Asher to claim it when the veil fell? Merlin had sacrificed himself to strengthen a veil he'd known would eventually come down. He'd had a plan. What was I missing? My mind spun. He'd left a piece of his soul and bound it to a set of enchanted daggers ... daggers that could cut through anything.

Anything.

Oh, God. I was such a fucking twit. The revelation sent a fresh surge of adrenaline coursing through my body.

"I got you, Ambrosius." I brought my arm up, dagger in hand, and sliced through the glowing connection. The tension eased, the pain ebbed, and then I was back in the forest of my dreams.

"It's time," my daimon whispered.

"Time for what?"

She pushed back the foliage, and I stepped into the clearing. The lake winked at me in the sun.

"Take it," my daimon said. "We have to take it now."

I looked into the shimmering water to see my face reflected back at me. And beyond that, beneath that, was the enticing glow. "What is it?"

"I can finally answer, because I finally know. It is salvation. Take it."

The water was cool against my fingertips, sliding up my hands, chilly and refreshing. The light began to rise to meet me.

"Harker!" Ryker shook me. "Breathe!"

Sweet air rushed into my lungs, and the world came back into focus.

Asher's bellow was a thing of beauty, but there was no time to revel, because the guards were lunging at us. Air slammed into them, knocking them off their feet. It looked like Ryker had his mojo back.

"Harker, you good?" he asked.

I pulled myself up, daggers at the ready.

"So good."

A guard aimed his gun at me.

"Don't hurt her!" Asher demanded.

The guard faltered, and it was all we needed. Ryker and I swung into action—him with his fists and me with my daggers.

"Stop them," Frederick screamed. "Get the girl!"

Fuck that. It was time for a distraction. I spun and slammed the blade back into the whirlpool. More light lanced out. And then the veil exploded, spilling shadows into the chamber.

Ryker grabbed my hand, and we ran.

I tugged Ryker toward the balcony we'd been standing on minutes before. "Can you get us up there?"

"What? Why?"

"Marika. We have to get her out."

His growl told me he wanted to argue, but there was no time. He swung me up into his arms, I tucked my head into the curve of his neck, and we were airborne. Exclamations and yells followed us as we took the route back down to the cells.

"Tell me we're going back because she might know how to get out of this maze," Ryker said.

"Yeah, that's exactly why." Or it was part of it, making it easier to justify the going back part. "I'm hoping she was conscious when they brought her here."

The cells came into view, and my daggers appeared, ready to slice through the lock. Less than five seconds and Marika was out. She didn't question how we were here, or what had happened. She didn't ask why we'd come back for her.

"This way." She turned and headed left, away from the balcony and farther into the maze. "There's a lift this way. It's how they brought me in."

"Where does it lead?" Ryker asked.

"Back into the tower. This whole fucking complex is underground. Under the tower. It stretches out for a block or two."

Bootfalls echoed around us. Behind us or in front, it was impossible to tell. The sound bounced around erratically. Marika skidded to a halt as we rounded a corner. Her hands shot up, and white light lanced out to hit a guard in the chest. His body convulsed and then he hit the ground.

Another hundred yards and the lift came into view, a metal rectangle snug in the stone wall. Marika hit the button and the whirr of the mechanism filled the corridor.

A quick glance over my shoulder to make sure the coast was clear. "How far down are we?"

She shrugged. "I'm not sure. But it's deep."

Fuck this and underground complexes in general. "How many of these lairs are there?"

"Lairs?" She snorted in amusement. "Yeah, I guess you could call them that, and I have no clue. This is our bunker, built decades ago by the first members of The Order. It's solid as shit, and if there was an apocalypse, then it could hold at least twelve hundred people. There are food stores and all sorts down here."

And a fucking rip in a veil to another world.

My scalp tingled. "They're coming."

Marika didn't ask who, she didn't need to, because two Order members came running around the corner and then broke into a sprint at the sight of us. My vision switched to aether-sight and their skin melted away to reveal the shades within. Their forms were lithe and corded with inky black muscle. They were taller than their hosts, wider too, and yet still contained.

Ryker fell into a defensive stance. Marika's hands erupted into white light, but there was only one way to get rid of the shades.

"Serenity, no!" Ryker's horror skimmed my spine, stabbing at the base of my neck. But it was too late. I was already in motion, hands out to meet skin, to expel the shades that had taken these bodies. The aether wrapped around me, ready to do my bidding, ready to tear out what didn't belong.

"No," Ambrosius said. "You were created for more than this. I remember it all." His voice was real and solid to my ears. "I took Arthur's weapons. I extracted the grace and I wove it into the fabric of the universe to sleep until the time was right, until it found the one — until it found *you*. Why tear out when you can annihilate? Use the power, Serenity. Become the weapon you were chosen to be."

His voice wasn't inside my head, it was outside. *He* was outside. My pulse lurched and then the lake from my dream filled my mind. The light ... the fucking light was a weapon. The power from Arthur's weapons, the weapons infused with God's grace. *I* was the weapon.

My body hurtled toward inevitable collision. The light beneath the water pulsed, once, twice, and then it exploded outward, slamming into my solar plexus and squeezing the air from my lungs. My hands made contact with flesh, and pure, unadulterated power poured out of my skin and into the hosts. Screams painted the air and then the shades exploded in a shower of ethereal embers.

"Harker?" Ryker sounded far away, so far away.

I stared at my hands, still glowing from within, then down at the two unconscious men. The shades were gone ... dead?

"This is who you are," Ambrosius said softly. "This is what I created. You are the weapon, Serenity. The only weapon we have."

"Where are you?"

"Run, Serenity. Run," he urged.

A tug on my arm urged me to my feet.

With Ryker's hand in mine, we ran for the lift, making it into the metal box. The doors slid shut, and we began to rise.

The lift spat us out into a tiny foyer with another reinforced door barring our way.

"We need to stop them from following us. Buy some time." My daggers cut through the electrics built into the wall, and the light on the lift button died.

"There are other exits," Marika said. "But not directly into this building." She led us through the door and into what looked like an old boiler room. Pipes and grills and vents and gloom greeted us.

"Quickly!" We climbed the stairs and exited into the main apartment foyer, directly into a fight. The sound of blades meeting blades and the fizz of power surrounded us. Hope and relief mingled and swelled in my chest at the sight.

Bane, Orin, Rivers, and Cassie fought back to back, taking on The Order members left behind to guard the tower. These were the expendable members of The Order, for surely Frederick would have known the MPD would come after us. He'd left these humans behind to die.

"Blood of my blood." Ambrosius's voice was a whisper in my ear. "My descendants. My blood."

I spun around to greet thin air.

"Stop!" Marika ordered. "Stop fighting. The Protectorate aren't our enemy. The enemy is below. You're fighting the wrong fight."

Her words washed over them with little effect on her people, but they caught the attention of the Protectorate. Relief flashed in Bane's eyes at the sight of us. He jerked his head toward the exit. Cassie, Rivers, and Orin were already maneuvering themselves toward the doors. Magic sailed over my head and singed the wall behind me.

"For fuck's sake! Move. I'll cover you," Marika yelled.

Ryker and I didn't need telling twice. Swords against power balls rarely worked out well. And if we had time, we could wait for them to exhaust their reserves of arcane power. But Asher and his shade army weren't going to run out of juice so easily, and even though I could kill them, there was no way I could take on all of them at once.

The doors buzzed open, and the night kissed my skin. Our van parked outside flared to life, and we piled in. Tires tore at tarmac and we were away. Safe. For now.

I crouched on the roof of the apartment block, fingers grazing the cold, wet ground. Rain fell in sheets, soaking through my clothes, seeping into my skin, and plastering my hair to my scalp. With one flick of my blades, I'd changed our world forever. I'd let in a new threat, one we knew nothing about. One we didn't understand, and my anchor, the only person that could help me work through it all, was no longer in my head. I'd called to him, begged him to explain what the fuck was going on, but all that greeted me was silence. By severing Ambrosius's link to his body, to Merlin's body, I'd somehow untethered him, and now he was gone. He'd left me with the knowledge of what I truly was, what he'd intended me to be all those centuries ago when he'd unmade Arthur's weapons. Those weapons were inside me. I was meant to kill the shades, to save us all. But I was just one person. One neph against an army. An army who could take on any face they chose. An army who'd taken Drayton. He was still alive inside. I knew it. But what now? Where did we go from here? This was big. Too big to contemplate. This wasn't the scourge or The Breed. This was alien and powerful and ancient.

Wings beat the air, and boots kissed the ground beside me.

"Harker, for fuck's sake. We've been looking for you everywhere."

"Do you see it?"

Bane curled his wing over me, shielding me from the downpour. "What do you see, Harker?"

I blinked, my vision switching into aether-sight. The night grew bright, and against the light floated the shadows, flying through the air, slamming into homes, slipping through the streets.

"I see them, Bane. I see them all."

The shades settled into homes, latching onto humans by seeping into the shadows they cast. This was the shades' entry point, and how the heck did you shield from that. Asher was building his army, an army that would eat away at the human psyche until it had control of the flesh. He'd come for us. Come for me, and come for Ambrosius, because without him, Asher wouldn't have full control of Merlin's power. Without Ambrosius, Asher would remain incomplete. Hide, my friend. Do not let him find you.

"We can do this, Harker," Bane said. "We can fight this."

"Yeah." I slipped out of aether-sight and looked into his rain-beaded face. "And when we do, we'll be fighting the whole of Midnight."

To be continued...

Serenity's journey continues in *Shades of Midnight*.

Check out the first chapter below.

"Harker, wake up!" Ryker's voice was saturated with urgency.

I shrugged off the arms of sleep and rolled onto my back, wiping drool from my chin. "Waaa?"

"Suit up, babe. We got a Code Shade."

I was instantly awake and alert. "Where?"

"Black Wing Mansion is under attack."

My body was already in motion—out of the bed and scrambling for the clothes I'd discarded on the floor. "Time?"

"Three in the morning."

Tidy hadn't been on my mind when I'd

crawled into bed less than two hours ago, and now my trousers were missing. Shit. "Where are the others?"

"We're meeting at the van," Ryker threw my slacks at me.

"Thanks." I pulled them on under my sleep-T and then gripped the edges of my shirt, ready to peel it off and stopped just in time.

Ryker averted his gaze. "I'll meet you downstairs."

The door shut behind him, and I scrambled to finish dressing. This was the fourth Code Shade this week—a term coined by yours truly. The last three had been sightings by our operatives trained in spotting the signs. The Deep had been hit first, and several nephs and humans had been infected. After that, two residential areas had been targeted, but I'd managed to expel the shades rooted inside the five humans who were showing symptoms of disorientation and aggression. I'd killed the shades in the humans whose souls had been completely devoured. We'd learned to distinguish between the two. Fully taken humans developed crimson irises, nephs didn't. For some reason, the shades couldn't mask this aspect in a human host like they could in neph body. So, red eyes equaled no human soul in residence. Killing a shade in a human host that still had his soul was not an option. In burning the shade up, I also burned through the soul. I swallowed recalling the time I'd killed a shade in a human host whose eyes hadn't turned yet—its screams had echoed alongside the shades as I'd burned it to a cinder. Now, the shades tended to scatter when I showed up—afraid I'd burn them out of existence, or expel them, but there was only one of me and hundreds of them. I couldn't keep this up forever, especially when they chose to hit two spots at the same time. Fuckers knew I couldn't be everywhere and neither could our officers.

Asher hadn't made a grab for me yet though, which was worrying. I'd killed two of his shades in the Order lair and many since, and yet, he'd stayed under the radar. I guess having the Order's wards all over the MPD building and grounds helped keep the big bad at bay, but still, I kinda just wanted to get it over with—for him to come for me and for me to kick his arse and be done with it. He was a shade just like the rest. So it stood to reason I should be able to kill him, right? It was probably why he was playing coy and sending his minions at me instead. Probably trying to tire me out, and sod, it was working, just not in the way he was probably hoping. Deciding to keep the shade presence in Midnight quiet, deciding to deal with it ourselves, was proving harder and harder with each attack.

My body was wrecked, out of balance, and simmering with power I wasn't sure how to control. It was growing faster than I could use it, expanding within me, leaving my skin itchy and tight. Expelling the shades didn't count, because for that I utilized my aether ability. The only thing that seemed to ease the discomfort was killing them. I hadn't even needed to feed for the past two weeks.

It's all right, we'll figure it out, my daimon reassured. Just like we'd figured out how her darkness had shrouded the light within me, and how my feeding had given her the power to keep my true nature hidden until the time was right. Now it was activated, there was no stopping it.

The others were bound to notice how it was affecting me soon. It was getting harder to hide the discomfort between exterminations. My body was a pressure cooker needing to blow off steam. Thank goodness the fuckers were attacking—I'd get to release some of the excess power. We were coping for now, my daimon and I. No point officially stressing until we had to. Right now, we had a Code Shade, and if they were hitting the Black Wings, then we'd be dealing with soulless hosts controlled by shades—the perfect chance for me to relieve some of the tension.

Zipping up my boots and grabbing my jacket, I headed out the door.

Marika and a couple of the Order of Merlin members met me in the foyer. Ryker was in the doorway, letting the cool night drift in and ruffle my hair. Marika's face was pale, and the dark smudges under her eyes spoke of lack of sleep.

"Sit this one out." I cupped her shoulder. "You may have access to the arcane, but your body is human."

He lips tightened. "If Ava and her unit can help, then so can we."

More Order members jogged into the foyer. This was their home for now, and thank God we had the space for them. They'd moved in after the shit had hit the fan a couple of weeks ago, and then Ava and her unit had moved in last week. The mansion was quickly becoming operations central, but it wasn't enough. We needed more boots on the ground. More help.

I sighed. "Fine, but then you need to get some sleep. Promise?"

She nodded, and gave me a half smile. "Okay, Mom."

We poured out of the mansion.

I'd never get completely used to the sensation of flying, especially when my defiance of gravity was dependent on another. Bane's arms were solid bands of steel around me. We were almost at the cliff house. I just hoped we got there on time. The van far below carried Orin, Cassie, River, and Ryker. Another three vans followed, filled with the rest of our officers, the Order members, Ava, and several of her unit.

If the shades were attacking the Black Wings, it meant they were confident in their numbers. It meant we were running out of time.

I was no fan of the winged but better the devil you know, right? The shades were aggressive and single minded, and who knew what their real agenda was. Asher had said that they had no grievance against humanity, that their issue was with God and the winged, but what was stopping them turning on us once the winged were gone? What was their end game anyway? It was unlikely they'd just sit back and chill out once their objective was achieved. Right now, the winged were the only thing standing between humanity and the shades.

"Your thinking is giving me a headache," Bane said. His breathe ruffled the hair at the nape of my neck.

We were flying with his chest to my back. I liked to get an aerial view. "I just hope we're in time to help."

His lips teased my earlobe. "The Black Wings are expert fighters. They won't go down easy."

I suppressed a shiver. "And the shades predate them. Who knows what they can do. They wouldn't be attacking if they couldn't hurt or even kill the Black Wings."

Bane was silent, which told me he had come to the same conclusion.

A horrific thought occurred to me. "You don't think the shades can infect the winged do you?"

"If they could do that, then why attack to kill them? They would have just taken the Black Wings as hosts. The message that came to me was clear. The shades were attacking to kill, and a dead host is a useless host."

Thank goodness he'd taken it upon himself to fill the rest of the MPD in about his relationship with the Black Wings, otherwise explaining how he'd known they were in trouble would have been awkward.

The screech of tires drifted up to us. We were losing altitude in preparation for landing.

"The others are in," Bane said. "It looks like the shades took down the gates. I'm going to drop you just inside. I need to get to the tower."

"The tower?"

"Abbadon needs me."

He was communicating with Abbadon again.

"Is he okay?"

"I don't know."

Below us, the ground was a sea of bodies in combat, Black Wings against humans and nephs, fifty against at least a hundred. Asher wasn't fucking around this time. He meant to take the Black Wings out of the picture tonight.

Time to kiss the ground. "Okay, do it. I'm ready."

Bane dropped me from a twenty-foot height. I hit the ground in a crouch and was up and running into the fray a split second later. Ryker's scent hit me from the left, and Rivers's from the right.

We surged toward the battle where Black Wings fought shades snug in neph and human skin: a young woman here, a teenager there, an old man, a young girl. It was disconcerting, and my feet faltered. The Black Wings must have been feeling the same distress because they were fighting, but not as hard as they probably could. They held back against the human hosts, their pledge to protect humans forcing them to pull their punches.

I switched to aether-sight, and the human skins melted away leaving only the powerful long limbed shades, inky black, crimson eyed and lethal. A Black Wing, right ahead of me, jumped back to avoid the swipe of a teenage girl's blade. He ducked and evaded while she slashed with the power of the shade she now was. There was no longer a human soul in that body, and the Black Wing needed to accept that and bloody fight back properly. There was nothing to save here, but he didn't know that. He couldn't see what I could.

The girl laughed. It was a tinkling sound that cut through the grunts and clanks of battle. She made, what would have been, a lethal strike, but I was already in motion, sliding between her and her target. Her eyes widened at the sight of me, the thing inside her recognizing me for what I was. I slammed my hand onto her face and blasted her with the divine power inside me. Yeah, my daimon and I had made that connection a week ago. Malphas had told me that the weapons had been made from a drop of God's grace, and if the power from the weapons was inside me then …

The shade screamed as it died, and the body of the girl dropped.

I rounded on the Black Wing. "There are *no* humans here. Just shades. Did you see her eyes? Crimson. The human soul is gone. You get that?"

His jaw tightened, and his eyes blazed with defiance, and for a moment I thought he'd strike me down, but then his wings unfurled, and he raised his head and bellowed. "Strike hard, strike true, there are no human souls here!"

It was as if his words had unlocked the phantom shackles holding the Black Wings back. Shrieks and battle cries rose up like angry smoke. The shades fell under sword and whip and blade, and I set to work, burning them to death with my power one by one while they were incapacitated. They couldn't die from their wounds, but what the Black Wings were doing was forcing them to consider retreat, and in the meantime, I was finishing them off.

I caught a glimpse of Malphas, his face

etched in steely determination as he parried against what had once been a Lupin. Shit. Lupins were higher level nephs, and this was the first one I'd seen infected by a shade.

Ryker appeared at my back, ready to swing his axe to ward off an attack by shades while I incinerated their brethren. Cassie and Orin worked together like a well-oiled machine in the periphery of my vision, and Rivers was to my far left, working back to back with a Black Wing while surrounded by shades inhabiting minor nephs. There was no hesitation on his part. Good.

My body burned with power as I took out enemy after enemy. Ryker swung his axe in an arc to force back a wave of shades. Black Wings surged forward to help but ended up cutting us off from each other.

I took out an old guy and then spun to counter the attack of another shade, but he skidded to a halt a meter away. I caught the flash of terror in his eyes as his attention went from the old guy's body and back up to me. He turned and ran. Nope. Not getting away. I broke into a sprint after him, leaped and tackled him to the ground. My hand closed on the nape of his neck and then he was gone, ash and cinder and death. The human shell relaxed beneath me. But there was no time to breathe because there was a shit load more of the fuckers to kill.

Something landed on my back, taking me

down, flattening me against the limp human body. Bones dug into my abdomen and chest, forcing the breath from my lungs.

"Shade killer. Now you die." The voice rasped in my ear.

A blade bit my skin, bringing tears to my eyes. My daimon roared in rage, and then a shadow was hurtling over my head, slamming into my attacker and taking him down. I scrambled up to see the shade that had attacked me pinned under Drayton. My heart slammed into my rib cage, hand coming up to stem the blood flow from the snick at my throat. He'd saved me ... Drayton was still in there. I'd been right!

"Alive!" Drayton slammed the shades head against the ground. "Asher wants her alive, you moron."

"I'm sorry, Xavier. I lost my head," the shade said

The bubble in my chest deflated. He wasn't saving me. Well he was, but not for the reasons I'd hoped.

Drayton climbed off the shade and stood to face me. He cracked his neck and smiled. And then he rushed me. It was unexpected, and my body froze for a fraction of a second too long. His hands wrapped around my waist, and then I was airborne for a fraction of a moment before slamming back down onto his shoulder, too winded to do anything but dangle like a sack of potatoes.

Fucking hell. He had me.

I twisted and bucked, but he was strong, too strong, and moving *way* too fast. Shit. Wait. This was my chance. I could expel the shade. Get it out of Drayton. I pressed my hand to his back and slipped into the aether. The skin beneath me morphed into the black sinewy body of a shade, larger than the average with power thrumming beneath its inky skin. This was … different. I delved, searching for a grip, but my ethereal hands slipped and slid against his essence.

His laughter echoed in my ears. "That won't work on me, shade killer. I'm a little too high up the food chain for you to expel. If you want me gone, you're going to have to kill me, and that would mean killing *him* too."

My pulse skipped and jumped. No. Drayton was gone. Xavier was lying now to save himself. I delved deeper, and brushed against something, small and bright and pulsing weakly,

Shit. My eyes pricked. Drayton. Oh, God.

The building rushed toward us. Xavier was taking me into the manor. Ryker? Where the fuck was he? Orin, Cassie, Rivers, anyone? But then we were inside the building, climbing stairs. What the fuck?

"Where are you taking me?"

"To Asher."

Shit!

Other books by Debbie Cassidy
The Gatekeeper Chronicles
Coauthored with Jasmine Walt
Marked by Sin
Hunted by Sin
Claimed by Sin

The Witch Blood Chronicles
(*Spin-off to the Gatekeeper Chronicles*)
Binding Magick
Defying Magick
Embracing Magick
Unleashing Magick

The Fearless Destiny Series
Beyond Everlight
Into Evernight
Under Twilight

Novellas
Blood Blade
Grotesque

The Shadowlands Series
Coauthored with Richard Amos
Shadow Reaper
Shadow Eater
Shadow Destiny

About the Author

Debbie Cassidy lives in England, Bedfordshire, with her three kids and very supportive husband. Coffee and chocolate biscuits are her writing fuels of choice, and she is still working on getting that perfect tower of solitude built in her back garden. Obsessed with building new worlds and reading about them, she spends her spare time daydreaming and conversing with the characters in her head – in a totally non psychotic way of course. She writes High Fantasy, Urban Fantasy and Science Fiction.

Connect with Debbie via her website at debbiecassidyauthor.com and also catch her on twitter -twitter@authordcassidy.

Made in the USA
Monee, IL
11 December 2023

48822073R00156